DRUNK WITH LOVE

ff

ELLEN GILCHRIST

Drunk With Love

faber and faber
LONDON · BOSTON

First published in the United States of America in 1986
by Little, Brown and Company, Boston
and simultaneously in Canada by Little, Brown and
Company (Canada) Limited, Toronto
First published in Great Britain in 1987
by Faber and Faber Limited
3 Queen Square, London WC1N 3AU

Printed in Great Britain by
Mackays of Chatham Ltd, Kent
All rights reserved

The characters and events in this story are fictitious.
Any similarity to real persons, living or dead, is
coincidental and not intended by the author.

British Library Cataloguing in Publication Data

Gilchrist, Ellen
Drunk with love.
I. Title
813'.54[F]   PS3557.I3426

ISBN 0–571–14671–6

389068

For Don and Roger, Compadres, Friends

"What has been overlooked is the irrational, the inconsistent, the droll, even the insane, which nature, inexhaustibly operative, implants in an individual, seemingly for her own amusement."

Albert Einstein

Contents

I

Drunk With Love

Drunk With Love

FREDDY HARWOOD sat in his office at his bookstore in Berkeley, California with his feet up on the desk and chewed the edge of his coffee cup. Frances came to the door three times to see if he would talk but he wouldn't even look at her. "You've got to send back those calligraphy books," she said. "We haven't sold a single one. I told you not to get that many."

"I don't want to send them back," he said. "I want them right where they are. Don't talk to me now, Frances. I'm thinking."

"Are you okay?"

"No. Now go on. Close the door."

"What's wrong?"

"Nora Jane's pregnant."

"Oh, my God."

"Leave me alone, Frances. Please shut the door."

"You need someone to talk to. You need — "

"Go run the bookstore, Frances. Please don't stand there."

She left the door open. Freddy got up and closed it. He laid his feet on a stack of invoices and stuck the edge of his thumb into his mouth. Manic-depressive, he decided. I was perfectly all right five minutes ago, a normal average neurotic walking down the street on my way to do my share of the world's work, on my way to add my light to the store of light, on my way to run the single most financially depressed bookstore in northern California and maybe the world. Perfectly, absolutely all right. Normal. And the minute I came in this room I started thinking about her and all she ever did in this room in my life was try to rob me. My God, I love her.

He raised his hands to his face. He made a catcher's mitt out of his hands and laid his face into that container. This is it, he decided, what all the science and art and philosophy and poetry and literature and movies were supposed to deliver me from and they have failed. A baby inside of her and it might not even be mine. A curved universe, low and inside, coming at me below the knees.

The first shock passed up the desk and through his hands and into his jaw. Books fell from their shelves, a chair slid into a window, there were crashes downstairs. She's in the car, he thought. She's in that goddamn convertible. He got up and pulled the door open and moved out into the hall. The stairway was still there. He ran down the stairs and found Frances in the History section holding on to a man in a raincoat. Several customers were huddled around the cash register. Willis and Eileen were on the floor with their arms over their heads. "Get out in the street," Freddy yelled. "For Christ's sake, get out of here. There's too much to fall. Let's go. Let's get outside." He pushed a group of customers through the turnstile. The second shock came. A section of art books fell across Children's Fantasy.

"Out the door," he was screaming. "For Christ's sake get out the door. Frances, get over here. Get out that door before it shatters." He dragged the customers along with him. They were barely out the door when the third shock came. The front window collapsed around the sign *Clara Books, Clara For Light*. His baby. The whole front window caved in upon a display of photography books. It moved in great triangular plates right down on top of Irving Penn and Ansel Adams and Disfarmer and David Hockney and Eugene Smith. A five-thousand-dollar print of "Country Doctor" fell across the books. "Is anyone else in there?" Freddy yelled. "Willis, where is Allison? Was she in the storeroom?"

"She's here," Willis said. "Right here by me." Telegraph Avenue was full of people. They were streaming out of the stores. A woman in a sari was running toward them. She grabbed Freddy's arm and pulled him toward a door. "In there," she was screaming. "My babies in there. You save them. In there." She pulled him toward the door of a restaurant. "In there," she kept saying, pointing to the door, pulling on his arm. "My babies in there. In the kitchen. In there." He pushed her behind him and walked into the restaurant. He moved between the tables, past the barstools and the bar, and turned into a narrow hall. He went down a hallway and into a kitchen and pushed a fallen counter out of his way and there they were, huddled beneath a sink, two little boys. He covered them with wet tablecloths and

picked them up, one under each arm, and walked back out
the way he had come. He handed them to a policeman and
sank down onto the pavement on top of a tablecloth and
began to cry. He rolled up in a ball on the wet white tablecloth and cried his heart out. Then he went to sleep. And
into a terrible dream. In the dream Nora Jane's retreating
back moved farther and farther away from him through
the length of Golden Gate Park. Come back, he yelled after
her, come back, I'm sorry I said it. I'm sorry. You goddamn
unforgiving, Roman Catholic bitch, come back. Don't you
dare break my heart, you heartless uneducated child. Come
back to me.

He woke up in a hospital room with his best friend, Nieman Bosley, standing beside his bed. Nieman was a film
critic for the *San Francisco Chronicle.* On the other side of the
bed was his mother. His hands were bandaged and there
were newspapers piled up on a tray. "You're a hero," Nieman said. "Coast to coast. Every paper in the U.S.A."

"My hands hurt," he said. "My hands are killing me."

"It's only skin," his mother said. "Stuart's been here all
night. He said they're going to heal. You're going to be all
right."

"Where is Nora Jane? Nieman, WHERE IS NORA
JANE?"

"She's on her way. She was on a bridge. She's in Sausalito with some plastic surgeon's wife."

"What day is it?"

"It's Friday. The city's a mess. It's the worst quake in
fifty years. Do you want some water?"

"She's pregnant. Nora Jane's going to have a baby.
Where is she, Nieman? I want to see her."

"She's coming. It's hard to get around right now, Freddy. She's on her way."

"Get me something for my hands, will you? Goddammit, where is Stuart? Tell him to get me some butter. You have to put butter on it, for Christ's sake. Mother, get Stuart in here. That bastard. Where is he? If he was all burned up I wouldn't be wandering around somewhere. Tell him to get me some butter for my goddamn hands." Stuart was a heart surgeon. He was Freddy's older brother. "I want some butter, for God's sake. Go tell him to get in here." A nurse appeared and slipped a needle out of a cone and put it into Freddy's arm and he drifted back down into his dreams. These dreams were better. It was the beach at Malibu on a windy day, the undertow signs were up and the sun was shining and everyone was sitting around under umbrellas drinking beer. Nieman was filming it. It was a movie about Malibu. They were going to make a million dollars by just being themselves on a beach telling stories and letting Nieman film it.

"She's pregnant?" Mrs. Harwood said, looking at Nieman. "His little girlfriend's pregnant?"

"It's been quite a day," Nieman said. "Well, your son's a hero," he added.

"Do you think his hands will be all right?"

"Medical science can do anything now."

Nora Jane Whittington was on the Richmond–San Rafael bridge when the earthquake moved across the beautiful city of San Francisco, California. She got out of her car and made her way around the front and climbed into a station wagon full of babies being driven by one Madge Johnson of Sausalito, California. After Nora Jane and

Madge were rescued by the Coast Guard they went to
Madge's house in Sausalito and Madge's husband, who was
a plastic surgeon, took everyone's pulse and the maid fed
them supper and Nora Jane told the Johnsons the story of
her life, up to and including the fact that she was pregnant
and wasn't sure if the father was Freddy Harwood or her
old boyfriend, Sandy. "You can have an amnio," Doctor
Johnson suggested. "That way you'll at least know if it's a
girl or a boy." He laughed at his joke.

"My God, Arnold, that's incredible you would joke at a
thing like this," Madge said. "I am really upset with you."

"That is how men face the facts of conception." Doctor
Johnson straightened his shoulders and went into his lec-
ture mode. "Men always get dizzy and full of fear and hi-
larity at the idea of children being conceived. It's a
phenomenon that has been documented in many cultures.
They have photographed men everywhere, including some
very remote tribes in New Guinea, being presented with the
fact that a conception has taken place and they uniformly
begin to joke about the matter, many going into this sort of
uncontrolled smiling laughing state. In much the same way
people are often filled with laughter at funerals. It seems to
be a clue to the darkness or fear of death hiding in us
all. . . ."

"Oh, please," Madge said. "Not now. About this amnio.
I think you should consider it, Nora. It would at least tell
the blood type."

"What exactly do they do?" Nora Jane said. "They stick
a needle down where the baby is? I don't like that idea.
How do they know where it is? I don't see how that could
be a good idea, to make a hole in there, a germ might get
in."

"Oh, they've got it all on a sonar screen while they're

doing it," Doctor Johnson said. "There's no chance a good technician would injure the baby. For your own peace of mind you ought to go on and clear this up. It's the modern world, Nora Jane. Take advantage of it. Well, it's up to you."

"Of course it's up to her," Madge said. "Let's turn on the television again. I want to see what happened in the city."

The television came on. Scenes of downtown San Francisco, followed by shots of firemen escorting people from buildings. There were broken monuments, stretchers, smashed automobiles. Then Freddy Harwood's face appeared, a shot Nieman had taken years ago at a Berkeley peace rally. "Bookstore owner walks into burning building," the announcer was saying. "In an act of unparalleled daring and courage a Telegraph Avenue bookstore owner walked into a Vietnamese restaurant and carried out two small children through what firemen described as an inferno. He was taken to Mount Sinai Hospital where he is being treated for burns of the hands and legs. The governor has sent greetings and in a press release the President of the United States said . . ."

"It's Freddy," Nora Jane said. "Oh, my God, Madge, that's him. How can I call him?"

Now Nora Jane stood at the foot of the hospital bed. Madge and Doctor Johnson were with her. Nieman had moved back. Mrs. Harwood was still stationed by her son's head. "He said you were going to have a baby," she said. "I think that's wonderful. I want you to know I will do anything I can to help." She lifted her hands. She held them out to the girl.

"How is he?" Nora Jane said. "Are his hands going to be okay?"

"They'll heal," Nieman said. "He's a hero, Nora Jane. He's gone the distance. That's the important thing. After you do that you can fix the rest."

"I don't know what to say," Nora Jane said. "I never knew a hero." She moved closer to the bed. She lay her head down on Freddy's crazy hairy chest. She very softly lay her head down upon his heart. He was breathing. No one spoke. Mrs. Harwood looked down at the floor. Madge rolled her hips into Doctor Johnson's leg. Nieman closed his mind.

"Nora Jane was a hero too," Madge said. "She helped me so much on the bridge. I never would have made it without her. I had a whole carpool with me."

"I didn't do anything," Nora Jane said. "I just came over there because I was afraid to be alone." She stood up, put her hand on Freddy's head, looked at his mother. She was thinking about something he did when he made love to her. He pretended he was retarded. "Oh, Missy Nora Jane, you so good to come and see us at the home," he would say. "Miss Dater, she say we should be so good to you. You want me to do what I do for Miss Dater? Miss Dater, she say I'm so good at it. She say I get all the cookies and candy I can eat. She say — "

"Shut up," Nora Jane would say whenever he started that. "I won't make love to you if you pretend to be retarded." Now that he was a hero she wished she had let him do it. She giggled.

"I'm sorry," she said. "I was just thinking about something he does that's funny. He does a lot of real crazy things."

"Don't tell me," Mrs. Harwood said. "I'm his mother."

"He's waking up," Nieman said. "Don't talk about him.

He can hear." Freddy opened his eyes, then closed them again, then waved his hands in the air, then moaned. He opened one eye, then the other. He was looking right at her. Nora Jane's heart melted. "Oh, Freddy," she said. "I'm so glad you're here."

"You're going to marry me," he said. He sat up on his elbow. "You are going to marry me, goddammit. You can't play with sombody's affections like that. I'm a serious man and SERIOUS PEOPLE GET MARRIED. Goddammit, my hands are killing me. Mother, would you get Stuart to come in here. That GODDAMN STUART, THEY OUGHT TO TAKE HIS LICENSE AWAY ... NORA JANE."

She put her hands on his chest. It seemed the best place to touch him. "I'll get a test," she said. "Doctor Johnson's going to fix it up."

"I don't want a test," he said. "I want you to marry me." He sank back down on the pillows. He was starting to cry again. Tears were starting to run down his face. His mother looked away. Nieman was writing it. I admire your passion, he was writing. I always admire passion. Freddy kept on crying. Madge and Doctor Johnson clutched each other. Nora Jane moved her hands up onto his shoulder. "Please don't cry anymore," she said. "You have a good time. You have a happy life. You watch movies all the time and read books and go up to Willets and camp out and build your solar house. Freddy, please stop crying. We're alive, aren't we? I mean, we're lucky to be alive. A lot of people got killed." He stopped at that.

"Wipe off my face, will you, Mother? And tell Stuart to get in here and put something on my hands. Oh, shit. Could I have another shot? I really want another shot."

"I love you," Nora Jane said. "I really love you, Freddy. I'm not just saying that. You are the best friend I've ever had."

"Good," he said. "I'm glad you do." Then the nurse came in the room with Freddy's brother right behind her and they moved everyone out into the hall and put him back to sleep.

Twelve injections of Demerol, seven days on Valium and Tylenol Number Three, four days on Bayer aspirin, failed attempts at transcendental meditation, self-hypnosis, and positive thinking, three days of walking all over the Mount Sinai Hospital behind the bookmobile, and Freddy was dismissed, with his hands still bandaged, to resume his normal life. Nora Jane picked him up at the emergency entrance. Three nurses helped him into the car, piling the backseat with flowers and plants.

"Stop off somewhere and get rid of these goddamn flowers," Freddy said, as soon as they pulled out onto the freeway. "I had to take them."

"I never saw anybody get that many flowers in my life, even when the archbishop died."

"Let's go to Peet's. I want a cup of real coffee so goddamn much."

"I made an appointment to get an amnio. They said I could come in tomorrow. I, well, never mind that."

"What? Never mind what? Cut down Redwood."

"I know. I was going to. Listen, I think you'll be sorry I did it. Well, anyway, what difference does it make?"

"It makes a difference to me."

"It might not even tell me anything. I don't even know what blood type Sandy is. Well, never mind it. I don't know how we got into this." She parked the car across from

Peet's and turned around in the seat and put her hands on his bandages. "I like you the most of anyone I've ever made love to or run around with. That's true and you know it. You're the best friend I've ever had. But I am not in love with you and that is also true." Her black curls were violet in the sun. Her shoulders were bare beneath the straps of her sundress. If he could not have her there was no reason for anything. If he could not have her there was no reason in the world, all was madness and random evil and stupid jokes being played by the galaxy and all its real and imagined gods. Gods, yes, if he could not have her there must be gods after all, only something in the image of man could be so dumb, mistaken, ignorant and cruel. The sun beat down on Nora Jane's blue convertible, it beat down on her head and shoulders and Freddy Harwood's bandaged hands. "You don't have to love me, Nora Jane. As long as that baby belongs to me."

"I don't think it does."

"Well, get out and let's go see if I can figure out a way to drink a cup of coffee without making a goddamn fool of myself." He knocked the door open with his elbow and stepped out onto Telegraph Avenue. Seven people were around him by the time Nora Jane could come around the other way. Three people who already knew and loved him and four more who wanted to. He's a hero, Nora Jane was thinking. Why would anybody like that want to like me anyway?

The next morning Nora Jane went down to the Berkeley Women's Clinic and had the amniocentesis. Afterwards she was going to meet Nieman and Freddy for lunch. She got up early and dressed up in a jade green silk dress, which was beginning to be too tight around the hips, and she screwed her face together and walked into the clinic determined to go through with it.

The first thing she had to do was take off the dress. Next she had to lie down on a bed surrounded by machinery, and in a moment she was watching the inside of her uterus on a television screen. "Oh, oh," the technician said. The doctor laughed.

"What happened?" Nora Jane said. "What's wrong?"

"There're two of them," the doctor said. "I thought so by the heartbeats. You've got twins." He squeezed her hand. The technician beamed, as delighted as if he had had something to do with it.

"What do you mean?" Nora Jane sat up on her elbow.

"Two babies in there. Identical by the looks of it. I think it's one sac. Can't be sure."

"Oh, my God."

"Be still now. Lie back. We're going to begin the amnio. It won't take long. It's all right. Don't worry. Hold Jamie's hand. Oh, that's a good girl." Then Nora Jane squeezed her eyes and her fists and the needle penetrated her skin and moved down into the sac Lydia and Tammili were swimming in and took one ounce of amniotic fluid and withdrew. The doctor secured the test tube, rubbed a spot on Nora Jane's stomach with alcohol and patted her on the leg. "You're a good girl," he said. "Now we'll get you out of here so you can celebrate."

"I can't believe it," she said. "I just don't believe it's true."

"We'll give you a picture to take home with you. How about that?" An hour later Nora Jane left the clinic carrying in her purse an envelope containing a photograph of Tammili and Lydia floating around her womb. This is too much knowledge, she decided. This is more than I need to know.

"What's this all about?" Nieman said. He was at an upstairs table at Chez Panisse holding Freddy's hand while the test went on. "Stop chewing your bandages, Freddy. Talk to me."

"She fucked this crazy bastard she used to go with in New Orleans. One afternoon when she was mad at me, so she doesn't know if the baby's mine. I should have killed him the minute I saw him. He's a goddamn criminal, Nieman. I ought to have him put in jail. Well, never mind, he isn't here anyway. So she's having this amniocentesis and she won't get the results for about a month anyway. I'm going crazy. You know that. Everything happens to me. You know it does. I'm probably going to lose my left hand."

"No you aren't. Stuart said it was healing. Besides, you're a hero. It was worth it."

"That's easy for you to say."

"So when will she find out?"

"I don't know. Who knows anything anymore. Well, I'm marrying her anyway if I can talk her into it. I can't live without her. You wouldn't believe how goddamn much my hands hurt at night. That goddamn Stuart won't give me a thing."

"Have you heard from the kids, the ones you saved?"

"Of course I have. They write me every other day. They've written me about ten letters. I'm going to get them into Camp Minnesota next year. I was thinking about that this morning. I'll take them up there as soon as they're old enough." Freddy still went to his old camp every summer. He was a senior counselor. Nieman looked away. Freddy's friends never mentioned his camp to him. They liked to talk about that behind his back. "Well," Nieman said. "Here she comes. You want me to leave?"

"Of course not, Nieman. This is Berkeley. Not Ohio. What's happening?" He stood up and held out a chair for Nora Jane and gave her a small quick kiss on the side of the face. Freddy was in extremely high gear this morning. Even for him he was running very tight and hot. He handed Nora Jane her napkin, laid it in her lap. "What did they say?"

"It's two babies. It's going to be twins. I have a picture of them if you'd like to see it." She fished it out of her purse and Freddy held it up to the light and looked at it.

"A month?" Freddy said. "Well, let's eat lunch. A month, huh? Thirty days."

"I don't think they're yours," she said. She was looking straight at him. "The right time of month when I was with Sandy. You never listen when I tell you that." Nieman coughed and drank his wine and signaled to the waiter for some more.

"The role of will is underrated in human affairs," Freddy said. "To tell the truth, Miss Whittington, you have driven me crazy. Have I told you that today?"

"I didn't mean to," she answered. "You're the one that thought up sleeping with me." Nieman rose a few inches from his chair and caught the waiter's eye. Nothing human is foreign to me, he said to himself, as he did about a hundred times a day.

II

Sandy, the beautiful and mysterious Sandy George Wade of Louisiana and Texas and nowhere. Abandoned when he was six years old, after which he roamed the world playing out that old scenario, doing things to please people and make them love him, then doing things to make them desert him. It was all he knew. One of the people he talked into caring for him was a drunken poet who taught English at his reform school in Texas. The poet taught him to love poetry and to wield it with his voice and eyes. Nora Jane was a sucker for poetry. When they lived together in New Orleans Sandy had been able to get her to forgive him anything by quoting Dylan Thomas or A. E. Housman or a poem by Auden called "Petition," which ends with a plea to "Look shining at, new styles of architecture, a change of heart." Nora Jane always took that to mean she was supposed to think anything Sandy did was all right with advanced thinkers like poets.

Now, on the same day that Nora Jane was having her amniocentesis, Sandy was sitting alone in his room in Mirium Sallisaw's tacky West Coast mansion thinking of ways to get Nora Jane to forgive him and take him back as her mate and child and live-in boyfriend. Sandy worked for Mirium Sallisaw in her cancer business. She sold trips to Mexico for miracle cures. She had made several million dollars collecting the life savings of terminal cancer patients and she paid Sandy well to be her driver.

In his spare time Sandy had been talking to Mirium's psychoanalyst and he was beginning to see that some of the things he had done might actually be affecting the lives of other people, especially and specifically Nora Jane, who was the best thing that had ever happened to him. He paced around his room and lay down on his bed and thought up a thousand tricks to get her back. Finally he decided to sit down and write out his frustration in a poem and have Mirium's Federal Express Service deliver it. By the time he had finished it he was so excited he abandoned the Federal Express idea and drove into town and delivered it himself. She was not there, so he left it in the mailbox.

Nora Jane found the poem when she got home from lunch at Chez Panisse. She had spent the afternoon arguing with Freddy about whether they should get married and finally, when she left him at his house, she had agreed to consider a trial marriage for the duration of her pregnancy.

Now she walked up onto the porch of the beige and green house where she had a room and saw the piece of paper sticking out of her mailbox. She knew what it was. No one in her life had left her things sticking out of mailboxes except Sandy. Sandy was one of the few young men left in the Western world who understood the power of written communications. There it was, sticking out and beckoning to her as she walked by the red salvia and the madrone hedge and the poppies. She pulled it out and sat down on the stairs to read.

Jane, Jane, where can you be?
Flown so very far from me.

The golden rain trees are blooming now
Above the house where we once lived.
Could we go there once again?
Could we recapture the love we had?

She folded it up and put it back into its envelope and went into the house and called him up.

"Come on over," she said. "I have a lot to tell you."

"What is that?" he answered.

"You won't believe it, I'm going to have two babies about six months from now."

"You mean that, don't you?"

"I think they're yours but I'm not sure. Are you coming?"

"As fast as I can get there."

"Do you think it's funny?"

"No."

"Neither do I."

He arrived at eight o'clock that night, pulling up to the curb in Mirium Sallisaw's white Cadillac Coupe de Ville. It was the car he used to drive her clients down to Mexico to the Laetrile clinic and to Las Vegas to get their bootleg Interferon. It was weird and depressing work and Sandy had been saving his money so he could quit. He was up to about four thousand dollars in savings on the night Nora Jane told him she was pregnant. He sped along the freeway thinking what a small sum it was, wondering where in the world he would get some more.

Nora Jane was waiting for him on the steps. He took her into his arms and the old magic was as good as new. The poem he had written to her was true. Back in New Orleans the golden rain trees were covering their old roof with golden dust. "That stuff is made of stars," Sandy had told her once. "And we are too."

"I love you," he told her now. "God, I've been missing you."

"I miss you too," she answered.

"I'm sorry I've been such an asshole. I don't know what makes me act that way."

"It's okay. It was half my fault. Come on in. I've got a lot to tell you."

It was some hours later and the moon was shining in on her small white bed with her new lace-trimmed sheets and the lace-trimmed pillowcases and the yellow lilies in a vase she had run out and bought when she knew he was coming. She was wrapped up in his arms. She had told him all she knew. Now she was finishing her speech. "I'm going to have them no matter whose they are. It's all I know for sure. I don't care what anyone says. Or who gets mad at me."

"Don't sound like that. I want them. I want them to be mine so much I'd reach inside and touch them." He ran his hands across her stomach. "Listen, baby, we're going to get out of here and get a place together and start living like white people. I've had all I can take of loneliness. You can call the shots. You tell me what you want and I'll deliver. I'm quitting Mirium. I've got four grand saved up in the bank and that will tide us over. I'm going to an employment agency tomorrow and see what they can offer. I'll take anything they offer me." He got up from the bed and pulled a package of cigarettes out of his pants and lit one and stood in the window smoking. The moonlight was on his body. He was so graceful it broke Nora Jane's heart to look at him. He was the most beautiful and graceful person she had ever watched or seen. Everything he did made sense in the beauty of movement department. Watching him now, so beautiful and perfect, she thought about a terrible story he told her about being left somewhere when he was small and standing by the door for days waiting for his mother to come back but she didn't come. "Oh, Sandy," Nora Jane got up and stood behind him, holding him in her arms. "I will never leave you again no matter what happens or what you do. I will stick by you if you want me to." Then she was crying tears all over his beautiful graceful back.

Across the campus of the University of California at Berkeley Freddy Harwood was in his hot tub getting drunk. His bandaged hand was propped up on a shoe rack and a bottle of VVSOP Napoleon brandy was by the soap dish and he was talking on the remote-control phone. "She hasn't even called and she isn't there. It means she's with him. I know it. She's bound to be. I've had it, Nieman. Life's not doing this to me. I'm getting out. I mean it. I'm getting into dope or moving to New York or paddling up to Canada in a birchbark canoe. None of it is funny anymore. The whole thing sucks and you know it. The whole show You goddamn well know it. I would take any age over this age. Fuck it all to goddamn bloody fucking hell. That's all I've got to say. I'm through."

Nieman said he would come over.

"Well, hurry up. I'm in deep, old buddy. I lost my sense of reality a while ago. I mean, I didn't do anything to deserve this. This is fucking unfair. I don't know. I just don't know."

Nieman said he was on his way. He called up Freddy's old girlfriend, Buiji Dalton, and told her to meet him there. Then he called a friend of theirs named Teddy who was a psychotherapist and told him to get in his car. They converged on Freddy's house. It was a wooden house with great glass wings that swept the horizon for miles across San Francisco and the bridges and the bay.

It had cost three hundred and fifty thousand dollars. It had paintings by every major painter who had worked in the United States in the last twenty years. It had books

in six languages and light and air and was full of food and
wine and bottled water from Missouri that tasted like
honey. In the middle of the patio, looking out on the bay,
was the hot tub where Freddy was contemplating suicide or
having a prefrontal lobotomy or taking heroin every day.
"The pain," he was saying into his tape recorder. "This is
real pain. This is not some figment of my imagination. This
is not just trying to get something that's hard to get. I don't
want her because she's hard to get. I want her because I like
to look at her and if those aren't my babies in there it's all
over, she will never marry me. I risked my life to save two
small children. I walked into a burning building. It isn't
fair. IT IS NOT FAIR. I'M MAD AS HELL AND I'M
NOT GOING TO TAKE IT ANYMORE." He turned off
the recording machine and called Nieman back. "You
haven't left yet?"

"I was going out the door."

"Have you got a tape of *Network*, that movie with Peter
Finch as the television announcer who gets all the people
yelling out the windows?"

"I think so."

"Bring it over, will you?"

Freddy laid down the phone and turned the recorder
back on. "Bitter," he said into the microphone. "Bitter, bitter, bitter, jaded, tired of life and cynical. No good for anything anymore. Nothing works. The system fucks."

Clouds of vapor were rolling in from the Pacific Ocean.
In a petri dish near the Berkeley campus Tammili and
Lydia Whittington's identical DNA began to give up its secrets to the Chinese student who was working overtime to
make money to bring his sister to the United States from

Singapore. "Very interesting," he thought. He added one drop of a chemical and watched the life below him form and re-form. *AB positive, universal donors,* he wrote on a pad. He translated it into Chinese with a few brief strokes of his pen. This case interested him very much. He wrote down the name, Nora Jane Whittington. Yes, when he got home he would cast the I Ching and see what else was in store for these baby girls with the lucky blood. Lin Tan, for that was his name, moved the dish to one side and picked up the next one.

Sandy got back into bed with Nora Jane and cuddled her up into his arms. He kissed her hair and then her eyes. He arranged their bodies so they fit against each other very comfortably and perfectly. He heaved a sigh. It was so fragile. It never stayed. It always deserted him. It always went away. It was here now. It would go away. It would leave him alone. "Calm down," she said. "Don't get scared. We don't have to be unhappy if we don't want to."

"When will you know?"

"They said a month. They're busy. So what kind of blood do you have anyway? I'm B positive."

"It's some weird shit. I've forgotten. I'll call and find out."

"Go to sleep. We'll make it."

"Do you love me?"

"Yes, I do."

"Well, I love you too."

Freddy got out of the hot tub. He was the color of a sunset at Malibu when there were plenty of clouds. Buiji Dalton took a big white towel and began to dry him off. She'd been trying to marry him for his money for five years and she wasn't giving up now. Not with all she had to offer. Not after she had divorced Dudley and only kept the house. "I couldn't believe it when I read it in the paper. I cut it out and showed it to everyone. I made a hundred copies and mailed them to people. I'm so proud of you."

"Hey, stop that, will you?"

"What?"

"Drying me. I'm okay. Come on. Let's go in the bedroom and watch this movie. It's the greatest movie made in the United States in four years and Nieman had to go and trash it. He trashed it. Wait till you see it. I want you to tell him what you think when it's over."

"Do you want anything to eat?"

"No, just get me that brandy, will you?" Freddy draped the towel over his shoulder and pulled the other part across his stomach to cover his reproductive organs and went into his bedroom and got into bed with his best friend and his old girlfriend on either side of him and pushed a button and the movie started. Freddy had changed his mind about suicide. After all, Nora Jane was practically illiterate. She had never even read Dostoevski. The copyright warning appeared on the screen. His psychiatrist friend, Teddy, came tearing into the room waving a bag from the deli. He took up the other side of Buiji Dalton and the movie began.

"This will go away," Sandy was saying. "It will disappear."

"It might not," Nora Jane answered. "Don't get scared. We don't have to be miserable if we don't want to be."

Down inside Nora Jane's womb Tammili signaled to her sister. "Nice night tonight."

"I wish it could always be the same. She's always changing. Up and down. Up and down."

"Get used to it. We'll be there soon."

"Let's don't think about it."

"You're right. Let's be quiet."

"Okay."

Nineteen Forty-One

RHODA was sitting on the front sidewalk trying to set some paper on fire with a magnifying glass. She was very worried at that time about what she would do if she was lost in the woods. It would be she and Dudley alone in the woods. Dudley would have the compass but he would not tell her what it said. He would sneak off while she was sleeping and leave her there to rot. She would not panic. She would not wander deeper into the woods. She would stay where she was until help came. She would find water. She would build a fire. But how to do it? Striking rocks on flint didn't work. How many times had she tried that? Rubbing sticks together didn't work. No, the best thing to do was carry a magnifying glass at all times.

Rhoda trained the glass on an ant crossing the sidewalk.

There were clouds in the sky. That was lucky for the ant.

"Get your things on," Dudley said, coming around the corner of the house, accompanied by his friend, Fat Tunney.

Fat Tunney hung back. Dudley squatted down by Rhoda. He was wearing his jodhpurs and his English riding hat. His leather riding crop was in his hand. You would never have believed he lived in Mound City, Illinois.

"Come on," he said. "Get dressed. Pop wants us to catch the horses. Fat Tunney's here. He'll help."

"I don't want to catch the damned old horses," Rhoda said. She trained the magnifying glass on Dudley's boots, thinking how nice it would be to give him a hotfoot. "I'm busy. Leave me alone."

"Come on. He wants us to saddle Dixie so you can go riding with this girl that's coming over. She's the banker's daughter."

"I don't want to go riding. You catch the goddamned old horses if you want to, since you're his slave. I'm not going back there and get in that goddamn old mud." Fat Tunney hung his head. He had never known a girl that talked like Rhoda. He had never known any people like the Mannings. They had been there six months. He didn't know what he did before they moved to Mound City. Every morning he woke up thinking about them and pulled on his clothes and went over to see what they were doing.

"That's right, Rhoda," he said now. "Your daddy said to tell you to hurry up."

"Well, I'm not going to," she said. "And get off the sidewalk. I'm killing ants."

"You better come on," Dudley said. He stood up. He was wearing his bandolier with his extra merit badges. He was

going for Eagle Scout. He was trying to be the youngest
Eagle Scout in America. "Get dressed," he said. "Don't
make me tell you again."

Rhoda trained the magnifying glass on his leg. "Go to
hell, you spy," she said. "Go back to Germany where you
belong. You aren't even a citizen. You're a yellow German
spy. You're really a Jap. That's why your skin's so yellow."
She was referring to Dudley's malaria. He had malaria
from living in a levee camp when he was small. The Mannings had lived a dangerous life. Everything happened to
them but they always recovered. They had too much char-
acter to give in to fate.

"Go back to Germany," Rhoda continued. "Go salute
the Führer. Go salute the Führer's bathroom." She cracked
up at that, beating her sandals against the sidewalk. "Go to
the German bathroom, go to the bathroom with the Japs.
Ha, ha, ha, Ha, ha . . ." She was laughing so hard it hurt.
Fat Tunney was laughing too but he was trying not to let it
show.

Dudley and Fat Tunney disappeared around the side of
the house. Rhoda got up and followed them. At the back of
the property was a corral surounded by a barbed-wire
fence. Little scalps of horsehair were stuck here and there in
the barbs. Little bloody pieces of Dixie and Cardinal and
Straw, the last two named for the colors of Rhoda's
mother's sorority.

As Rhoda came up the horses were milling around the
water tank, bumping each other's flanks, slurping water,
making noises. Rhoda didn't trust them. They were different from horses in books, good faithful creatures like Black
Beauty or beautiful white stallions running across the
plains carrying the mail. These were quarter horses and

their only purpose in life was to teach Rhoda and Dudley not to be afraid.

"Get your jodhpurs on, honey," her father said. He was sitting on the gate. "Mr. Trumbo is bringing his little girl over here to ride."

"I can't," she said. "I'm menstruating."

"Oh, my God," he said, and climbed down off the fence, hoping to get to her before she said it again and the boys heard it. "ARIANE," he screamed toward the house. "ARRIIIIIANNNEEE, get out here and get this child. Who told you that?" he demanded, taking her by the arm. "Who told you a thing like that?" His face was as red as the sun. Rhoda's mother came running out of the house and across the yard and swooped her up. "Where does she learn those things?" he was saying. "Who told her that? Who told her such a thing?"

"Sherry Nettleship's aunt told us all about it," Rhoda said. "You can't ever go swimming and blood runs down your legs. And you can't ride horses or anything like that. I've been doing it all morning. There's blood all over the sidewalk. Go look for yourself." It was an inspiration. Actually, Rhoda had spilled red Kool-Aid while she was making fire. That was what had drawn the ants. "You can die if you aren't careful," she continued. "Anything can happen when you menstruate."

Rhoda's mother took her into the house and put her in the bathtub. She knelt beside the tub looking down at Rhoda's plump apricot-colored legs, her little precious vagina, her soft round stomach, her navel, where this maddening child had actually been joined to her own body. She dripped water from her hands over Rhoda's legs. She touched her hair. She allowed her hand to rest on Rhoda's skull. Ariane Manning loved her children so much it took her breath away to touch them. A little girl, a precious sweet baby girl, her little girl, her daughter.

"Don't ever talk about that again," she said. "We don't talk about things like that. It is a long, long time before that will happen to you. When the time comes I will tell you what to do. It's a long way off, a lot of years. I can't believe Mrs. Nettleship told you a thing like that. I just can't believe it."

"She was drunk," Rhoda said. "She was drinking bathtub gin. She told us everything about it. She told me and Sherry everything there is to know."

"Oh, my God," Ariane said. "I can't believe it. I just can't believe we're in this town. Oh, my God. I just don't know. I just don't know where to start."

She took her daughter from the tub and dried her with a blue towel and dressed her in jodhpurs and a white blouse and a little checked vest. She held the boots while Rhoda wiggled her feet into them. She brushed Rhoda's hair. She dotted her neck with perfume. Stuck a handkerchief in her pocket. She stopped crying. She got a hold on herself.

When Rhoda got back to the corral the horses were saddled. Dudley and Fat Tunney were just saddling the last one, a large black and white mare named Dixie. They were tightening up the cinches. Dixie was fighting them, puffing up her belly, kicking, carrying on.

She is the worst horse we have, Rhoda thought. I bet he's going to make me ride her.

"Get on Dixie, Sister," her father called out from his command position astride the gate. "Let the boys have the geldings."

"She doesn't have any gaits," Rhoda said. "I can't stand to ride a horse that doesn't have gaits."

"You wouldn't know what to do with gaits," Dudley said. "You can hardly even ride."

"Shut up all that arguing," her father said. "Give her a leg up, Fat Tunney. Look out! Here's our company coming in the back." Rhoda swung herself up into the saddle. A languid, droopy-looking girl on an Appaloosa was turning into the yard from the road behind the place. Rhoda looked her over. She didn't look like much. She was barely even holding the reins as the horse came plodding over. Still, she was a banker's daughter. She might have a playhouse or a chauffeur or anything. "Hello," Rhoda said, as soon as the girl was near enough to hear. "I'm Rhoda."

"Well, I'm Lelia," the girl said. "I'm supposed to show you where to go."

"This is Mr. Trumbo's daughter," her father said. "That's been so nice to me. Now you girls go on and have a ride and when you get back I'll take us out for ice cream. Use your knees, Sweet Sister. Don't forget to use your knees."

"I can't feel anything through this saddle. This saddle's too thick."

"Well, don't complain about everything. Go on, then, you girls get going before it gets too hot." He climbed down off the fence and took the bridles and led the horses down the path and turned them in the direction of the road. "Ride 'em now," he said. "Show him who's boss. Let's see you ride."

Lelia's Appaloosa began to trot along the path, a nice clean little trot. Rhoda dug her knees into the saddle. She straightened her back. She had a vision of herself riding through the town, her hair flying back from her face, the eyes of the town following her, worshipping and jealous.

She dug her heels into Dixie's side. She pulled on the reins. The horse balked. Rhoda tried again. This time she jerked Dixie's head from side to side. Slapping the reins against her neck. "Get going," she said. "Come on, you goddamn old horse."

Dixie lowered her head, then rose up on her hind feet and spun in a circle. She hit the ground, then took off for the road. Rhoda clung to the reins, then clung to the mane. The horse jumped a ditch. The saddle moved, then moved again. Rhoda's head was on a level with Dixie's thighs. Her eyes were on the road.

Dixie turned and began to run along the railroad tracks. A man ran out of a house and tried to flag them down. "Let go," he yelled. "Let go. Let go and fall."

Her head hit the tracks. Then hit again. There was grass and steel and sky. Then there were faces.

Her father was there and Mr. Samuels and they put her into a car and she was going somewhere. For a long time she was going somewhere. Her grandmother seemed to be in the car, opening a suitcase, getting out presents. Her beautiful tall grandfather was there, wearing a gray suit. He was holding her head in his hands. His great blue eyes were sad. He took her into his old wicker rocking chair. He read to her from magazines. He let her smoke his pipe. He gave her money. Many quarters and nickels and dimes. As soon as the store opened she could put them in the slot machine. The slot machine was in the car. It was a Buick with a slot machine. She and her grandmother and grandfather would ride forever sticking money in the slot machine. Nickels poured out onto the seat. They had so many nickels they didn't know what to do with all of them. They threw them out the windows so the poor people could have some and play their own slot machines. The poor people caught the nickels. They held them up to the light.

When Rhoda woke up she was in her own bed and her mother was sitting beside her and Doctor Finley was there and her name was in the newspaper.

Rhoda Katherine Manning, only daughter of Chief Engineer Manning of the U.S. Corps of Engineers, is recovering from a fall she received when the horse she was riding ran away. She received cuts and bruises and is recovering at the Manning home on Maple Street.

"I'm going to kill that horse," she said, opening her eyes, lifting her head from the pillow.

"Your father already beat it half to death," her mother said. She sighed and looked away.

"You made me do it," she said, seeing him standing in the door. "You made me ride it. And Dudley put the saddle on. He did it wrong. He didn't put the saddle on right." Dudley was standing at the foot of the bed, looking thin and yellow. "You did it," she said. "You tried to kill me."

"Don't talk like that, Rhoda," her mother said. "It was an accident. It wasn't anybody's fault."

"It was his fault," she said, sitting up higher. "He and Fat Tunney. They did it. The saddle came off. That's why I fell. You did it," she said, looking right at him. "You did it on purpose. You tried to kill me so you can inherit everything."

"Come on, son," her father said. He put his arm around his son and led him from the room. "Let your mother take care of her."

"He did it," she yelled after them. "I almost died. It's a wonder I'm not dead."

"Let me get you some supper," her mother said. "Everyone in town's been bringing food. There's quail with a glass cover and chocolate custard and everything you love."

"I dreamed about Dan-Dan," Rhoda said. She sank back into the pillows, allowing her mother to hold her hands. "I dreamed Dan-Dan and Big Daddy and I were going to sleep in those concrete wigwams where we stayed that other time. Did you tell them yet? Do they know I almost died?"

"They're on their way," her mother said. "They ought to be here soon."

"Good," Rhoda said. "I'll get them to kill the horse."

The Expansion of the Universe

IT WAS SATURDAY AFTERNOON in Harrisburg, Illinois. Rhoda was lying on the bed with catalogs all around her, pretending to be ordering things. It was fall outside the window, Rhoda's favorite time of year. "The fall is so poignant," she was fond of saying. This fall was more poignant than ever because Rhoda had started menstruating on the thirteenth of September. Thirteen, her lucky number. Rhoda had been dying to start menstruating. Everyone she knew had started. Shirley Hancock and Dixie Lee Carouthers and Naomi and everyone who was anyone in the ninth grade had started. It was beginning to look like Rhoda would be the last person in Southern Illinois to menstruate. Now, finally, right in the middle of a Friday night double feature at the picture show, she had started. She had stuffed some toilet paper into her pants and hur-

ried back down the aisle and pulled Letitia and Naomi
back to the restroom with her. They huddled together, very
excited. Rhoda's arms were on her friends' shoulders. "I
started," she said. "It's on my pants. Oh, God, I thought I
never would."

"You've got to have a belt," Letitia said. "I'm going
home and get you a belt. You stay right here."

"She doesn't need a belt," Naomi said. "All she needs is
to pin one to her pants. Where's a quarter?" Someone pro-
duced a quarter and they stuck it in the machine and the
Kotex came sliding out and Rhoda pinned it inside her
pants and they went back into the theater to tell everyone
else. *A Date with Judy*, starring Elizabeth Taylor, was playing. Rhoda snuggled down in her accustomed seat, six rows
from the front on the left-hand aisle. It was too good to be
true. It was wonderful.

It was almost a week later when her mother discovered
what had happened. Rhoda tossed the information over
her shoulder on her way out the door. "I fell off the roof last
week," she said. "Did I tell you that?"

"You did what? What are you talking about?"

"I started menstruating. I got my period. You know, fell
off the roof."

"Oh, my God," Ariane said. "What are you talking
about, Rhoda? Where were you? What did you do about it?
WHY DIDN'T YOU TELL ME?"

"I knew what to do. I was at the picture show. Naomi
gave me some Kotex."

"Rhoda. Don't leave. Wait a minute, you have to talk to
me about this. Where are you going?" Rhoda's mother
dropped the scarf she was knitting and stood beside the
chair.

"I'm going to cheerleader practice. I'm late."

"Rhoda, you have to have a belt. You have to use the right things. I want to take you to Doctor Usry. You can't just start menstruating."

"We're going to get some Tampax. Donna Marie and Letitia and I. We're going to learn to wear it." Then she was gone, as Rhoda was always going, leaving her mother standing in a doorway or the middle of a room with her jaw clenched and her nails digging into her palms and everything she had believed all her life in question.

Now it was October and Rhoda was lying on the bed among the catalogs watching the October sun outside the window and getting bored with Saturday afternoon. She decided to get dressed and go downtown to see if Philip Holloman was sitting on his stool at the drugstore. Philip Holloman was a friend of Bob Rosen's and Rhoda was madly in love with Bob Rosen, who was nineteen years old and off at school in Champaign-Urbana.

Bob Rosen was the smartest person Rhoda had ever known. He played a saxophone and laughed at everything and taught her how to dress and about jazz and took her riding in his car and gave her passionate kisses whenever his girlfriend was mad at him. She was mad at him a lot. Her name was Anne and she worked in a dress shop downtown and she was always frowning. Every time Rhoda had ever seen her she was frowning. Because of this Rhoda was certain that sooner or later Bob Rosen would break up with her and get his pin back. In the meantime she would be standing by, she would be his friend or his protégée or anything he wanted her to be. She would memorize the books and records he told her to buy. She would wear the clothes he told her to wear and write for *The Purple Clarion* and be a

cheerleader and march with the band and do everything he
directed her to do. *So he would love her.* Love me, love me,
love me, she chanted to the dark bushes, alone in the yard
at night, sending him messages through the stars. Love me,
love me, love me, love me.

Rhoda walked down Rollston Street toward the town,
concentrating on making Bob Rosen love her. She walked
past the ivy-colored walls of the Clayton Place, past the
new Oldsmobile Stephanie Hinton got to drive to school,
past the hospital and the bakery and the filling station. The
Sweet Shop stood on its corner with its pink-and-white gin-
gerbread trim. I could stop off and get a lemon phosphate
before I go to the drugstore, Rhoda thought. Or one of
those things that Dudley likes with ice cream in the lemonade. There was something strange about the Sweet Shop.
Something spooky and unhealthy. Rhoda was more com-
fortable with the drugstore, where the vices were mixed in
with Band-Aids and hot water bottles and magazines and
aspirins.

Leta Ainsley was in the Sweet Shop. Leaning up against
a counter with her big foreign-looking face turned toward
the door. She had been in Japan before she came to Harrisburg. She had strange ideas and hair that grew around her
lips. She was the Junior editor of *The Purple Clarion* where
Rhoda was making her start as a reporter. She had let
Rhoda wear her coat and her horn-rimmed glasses when
the photographer came to take a picture of *The Purple Clarion* staff for the yearbook.

"I'm glad you're here," Leta said, drawing Rhoda over to
a table by the window. "You wouldn't believe what happened to me. I've got to talk to someone."

"What happened?" Rhoda moved in close, getting a whiff of Leta's Tabu.

"I've been, ahh, in a man's apartment." Leta paused and looked around. She bent near. The hairs above her lip stood out like bristles. Rhoda couldn't take her eyes off them. Leta was so amazing. She wasn't even *clean*. Rhoda raised her eyes from Leta's lips; Leta's black eyes peered at her through the horn-rims. "I've been dryfucking," she said very slowly. "That's what you call it."

"Doing what?" Rhoda said. A shiver went over her body. It was the most startling thing she had ever heard. People in Harrisburg, Illinois were too polite to talk about something as terrible and powerful as sex. They said "doing it" or "making babies," but, except when men were alone without women, no one said the real words out loud.

"Dryfucking," Leta said. "You do it with your clothes on."

"Oh, my God," Rhoda said. "I can't believe it."

"It feels so wonderful," Leta said. "I might go crazy thinking about it. He's going to call me up tomorrow. He's coming to band practice on Tuesday night and see us march. I'll show him to you."

"Good," Rhoda said. "I can't wait to see him."

"What you do," Leta went on, taking a cigarette out of its package without lifting her elbows from the table. "Is get on a bed and do it. You need a bed." Rhoda leaned down on the table until her head was almost touching Leta's hands. The word was racing around her head. The word was unbelievable. The word would drive her mad.

"I have to go up to the drugstore and look for Philip Holloman," she said. "You want to come with me?"

"Not now," Leta said. "I have to think."

"I'll see you tomorrow then," Rhoda said. "I'll turn in my gossip column stuff before class. I've almost got it finished. It's really funny. I pretended Carl Davis was Gene Kelly and was dancing in Shirley Hancock's yard."

"Oh, yeah." Leta sat back. Unfurled herself into the chair. "That sounds great."

"I'll see you then."

"Sure. I'll see you in the morning."

Rhoda proceeded on down the street, past the movie theater and the cleaners and the store where Bob Rosen's unsmiling girlfriend sold clothes to people. Rhoda considered going in and trying on things, but she didn't feel like doing it now. She was too haunted by the conversation with Leta. It was the wildest word there could be in the world. Rhoda wanted to do it. Right that very minute. With anyone. Anyone on the street. Anyone in a store. Anyone at all. She went into the drugstore but no one was there that she knew, just a couple of old men at the counter having Alka-Seltzers. She bought a package of Nabs and walked toward the park eating them, thinking about Leta and band practice and men that took you to apartments and did that to you. The excitement of the word was wearing off. It was beginning to sound like something only poor people would do. It sounded worse and worse the more it pounded in her head. It sounded bad. It made her want to take a bath.

She went home and went up to her room and took off her clothes and stood in front of the full-length mirror inspecting her vagina. She lifted one foot and put it on the doorknob to get a better look. It was terrible to look at. It was too much to bear. She picked up her clothes and threw them under the bed and went into the bathroom and got into the tub. She ran the hot water all the way up to the drain. She lay back listening to the sucking noises of the drain. Dryfucking. She sank down deeper into the water. She ran her hand across her stomach, found her navel, explored its folds with her fingers, going deeper and deeper, spiraling down. It was where she had been hooked on to her mother. Imagine having a baby hooked on to you. Swimming around inside you. It was the worst thing that could happen. She would never marry. She would never have one swimming in her. Never, never, never as long as she lived. No, she would go to Paradise Island and live with Queen Hippolyta. She would walk among the Amazons in her golden girdle. She would give her glass plane away and never return to civilization.

"Rhoda, what are you doing in there?" It was her real mother, the one in Illinois. She was standing in the doorway wearing a suit she'd been making all week. Dubonnet rayon with shoulder pads and a peplum, the height of style. "You're going to shrink."

"No, I'm not. What was it like to have me inside of you? How did it feel?"

"It didn't feel like anything. I've told you that."

"But it was awful when I came, wasn't it?"

"You came too fast. You tore me up coming out. Like everything else you've ever done." Ariane drew herself up on her heels. "You never could wait for anything."

"I'm not going to do it," Rhoda said. "You couldn't pay me to have a baby."

"Well, maybe no one will want you to. Now get out, Rhoda. Your father's bringing company home. I want you dressed for dinner."

"How far in does a navel go?"

"I don't know. Now get out, honey. You can't stay in the tub all day."

Rhoda got out of the tub and wrapped herself in a towel and padded back to her room.

"Hello, Shorty," Dudley said. He was standing in the doorway of his room with a sultry look on his face. His hands were hooked in the pockets of his pants. He filled the doorframe. "Where you been all day?"

"None of your business," she said. "Get out of my way."

"I'm not in your way. We're going to move again, did you know that?"

"What are you talking about?"

"He's buying some mines. If he gets them we have to move to Kentucky. I was at the office today. I saw the maps. He's going to make about a million dollars."

"You don't know what you're talking about."

"You wait and see."

"Shut up. He wouldn't make us move in the middle of high school."

"He might have to."

"You're crazy," she said, and went on into her room and shut it out. She had gone to four grade schools. She was never going to move again. She was going to live right here in this room forever and wait for Bob Rosen to take his pin back and marry her. "He's crazy," she said to herself and pulled her new pink wool dress off the hanger and began to dress for dinner. "He doesn't know what he's talking about."

Monday was a big day at Harrisburg High School. They were taking achievement tests. Rhoda liked to take tests.

She would sharpen three pencils and take the papers they handed her and sit down at a desk and cover the papers with answers that were twice as complicated as the questions and then she would turn the tests in before anyone else and go outside and sit in the sun. Rhoda considered achievement test day to be a sort of school holiday. She went out of the study hall and past the administrative offices and out the main door.

She sat in the sun, feeling the October morning on her legs and arms and face, watching the sunlight move around the concrete volumes of the lions that guarded the entrance to Harrisburg Township High School. The Purple Cougars, Harrisburg called its teams. It should be the marble lions, Rhoda thought. I ought to write an editorial about that. He told me to write editorials whenever I formed an opinion. She imagined it, the lead editorial. Not signed, of course, but her mark would be all over it. Her high imagination. He still got the paper up in Champaign-Urbana, since he had been its greatest editor.

She picked up her books and hurried into the school and up the broad wooden stairs to the *Purple Clarion* office. She sat down at a table and pulled out a tablet and began to write.

I was out in the October sun getting tanned around my anklets when it occurred to me that we have been calling our teams the wrong name. Purple Cougars, what does that mean? There aren't any cougars in Harrisburg. No one even knows what one is. When we try to make a homecoming float no one knows what one looks like. Everyone is always running around with encyclopedias in the middle of the night trying to make a papier-mâché cougar.

WE SHOULD BE THE MARBLE LIONS. Look at what is out in front of the school. JUST GO AND LOOK ...

"What you doing, Scoop? I was just looking for you." It was Philip Holloman.

"Oh, God, I've got this great idea for an editorial. Leta said I could write one whenever I got in the mood. You want to hear it?"

"I have a letter for you." He was wearing his blue windbreaker. He looked just like Bob Rosen. They had matching windbreakers, only Bob's was beige. She had been in the arms of Bob Rosen's beige windbreaker and here was Philip's blue one, not two feet away. He was holding out a letter to her. A small white envelope. She knew what it was. At her house there were three of them wrapped in blue silk in the bottom of her underwear drawer.

"Why did he write me here?"

"I don't know. Look at the address. Isn't that a kick? God, I miss him. I miss him every day." She took the letter. *To,* Miss Scoop Cheetah, R.K. Manning, Ltd., *The Purple Clarion,* Harrisburg Township High School, Harrisburg, Illinois.

In the left-hand corner it said: Rosen, Box 413, University of Illinois, Champaign-Urbana, Illinois.

Rhoda took the letter and held it in her hand, getting it wet from her palms, and left her notebook on the table with her editorial half-finished and excused herself, breathing, still breathing, barely breathing, and went out into the hall. Philip watched her from the vantage point of eighteen years old. He liked Rhoda Manning. Everyone that knew her liked her. People that understood her liked her and people that thought she was crazy did too. Rosen was going to direct her career and someday marry her. That was clear. Anybody could see what was going to happen. She was on her way. She was going to set Harrisburg Township High School on its ear. Rosen had decreed it.

Dear Cheetah, [the letter began. Rhoda had found a quiet place in the abandoned lunchroom.]

I am going to be home this coming weekend. November 1, 2, and 3. If you will be waiting for me wearing a black sweater and skirt and brown shoes and get that hair cut into a pageboy I'll be over about 6:30 to take you to the ball game in Benton. If you have to wear your cheerleading things (Is there a freshman-sophomore game that night?) you can bring the black skirt and sweater and change at my cousin Shelton's house.

If you show up in that pink dress looking like Shirley Temple you will have to find someone else to violate the Mann Act with. I have been thinking about you more than seems intelligent.

Things aren't going well up here now. I have had to miss a lot of classes and will have to go to Saint Louis on the 4th for some more surgery. Mother is coming from Chicago. Tell Philip. I left it out of his letter.

Did you read that style book I sent you? You *must* study that or no one will ever take your pieces seriously. Leave the feature section to the idiots. We are after news.

> Love,
> Bob

She went home that afternoon and took the other letters out of their drawer and got up on her bed and read them very slowly, over and over again.

Dear Cheetah,

I made it to Champaign-Urbana in the midst of the worst winter storm in history. They want me. They took me over and showed me the Journalism Department. You wouldn't believe how many typewriters they have. It must be twenty.

Coleman Hawkins is going to play here next week. Stay away from those Nabs. See you soon. In a hurry.

> Love,
> Bob

Dear Cheetah,

My roommate brought a cake from home and a cute habit of picking his nose when he studies. The classes look like a snap except for Biology which is going to require "thought and memory." This Williard guy teaching it has decided that science will save the world and I am going to sit on the front row and keep him from finding out I'm a History major. If at all possible.

Mother cursed out the Lieutenant Governor of Illinois at a street corner. Where in the hell do you think you're going, she was muttering and I looked at the license plate and it said 2.

Remember what I told you about those tryouts. Team up with Letitia and don't think about anything but the routine. And remember what I told you about talking to Harold about writing the play. You can do it if I did.

Big kisses,
Bob

Dear Cheetah,

I was sick in bed for two days and still can't go to class. I've memorized everything in the room including the nose-picker's daily Bible study guide. Here's his program for the day.

FOR SEPTEMBER 29

DO'S AND DON'TS

Do decide that those in power are there to take care of you. Do listen when they speak for they are there by the will of the Lord for your benefit. Honor the ones the Lord has put over you to help you on the way to your recovery from the sickness and disease of ignorance of the Lord.

Don't be one of those that question the wisdom of older people. Sit at the feet of your parents and teachers. Let love be on our face and shine unto them the light of the Lord.

Don't let vice call out to you. The devil is everywhere. Be on the lookout for his messengers. Do not be fooled by smiles and flattery.

The nosepicker suspects me of being in the legions of the devil. He has asked to be transferred to another room. If the devil *is* on my side that will happen soon. I cough as much as possible and ask him what the Bible is and try to get into as many conversations as possible tidbits about my mother's notoriously filthy mouth. I can't wait till you meet her. She is coming to Harrisburg this summer to stay with grandmother and me.

I'm tired a lot but it's better. Write me. I love your letters and get some good laughs.

What is happening about the play? What did Harold say?

Love,
Bob

Dear Cheetah,

Back in class. Your letter came Monday. That's great about the play. I think you should call it Harrisburg Folly's, not Follies. Or something better. We'll work on it when I'm home Christmas.

Why skits? How many? Too busy to make this good. Hope you can read it. Out the door.

Bob

That was it. The entire collection. Rhoda folded them neatly back into their creases and put them in their envelopes and wrapped them in the silk scarf and put them beside the bed on the table. Then she rolled the pillow under her head. He's coming home, she said to herself as she cuddled down into the comforter and fell asleep. He is coming home. He's coming over here and get me and take me to Benton to the game. I'm not eating a bite until Friday. I will eat one egg a day until he gets here. I'll be so beautiful. He will love me. He'll do it to me. He doesn't even know I started. I might tell him. Yes, I'll tell him. I can tell him anything. I love him. I love him so much I could die.

Then it was Tuesday, then it was Wednesday, then it was an interminable Thursday and Rhoda was starving by the time she dragged herself home from school and went into the kitchen and boiled her daily egg.

"You are going to eat some supper, young lady," her mother said. "This starvation routine is going to stop."

"I ate at school. Please leave me alone, Mother. I know what I'm doing."

"You look terrible, Rhoda. Your cheeks are gaunt and you aren't sleeping well. I heard you last night. And I know what it's about."

"What's it about? What do you know?"

"It's about that Jewish boy, that Rosen boy you're going to go to Benton with. I don't know about your driving over there with him all alone, Rhoda. Your father's coming home tomorrow night. I don't know what he's going to say."

"Philip Holloman and Letitia's sister, Emily, are driving over with us. I mean, he's the editor of the paper. That ought to be enough chaperones. Emily's going. You call her mother and see." If her mother did call, Rhoda would have to try something else. "Call Emily's mother and see. We're going together. The ex-editor of my newspaper I happen to write for and the editor this year and Letitia's sister. I guess that's enough for anybody. I am so lucky to get to go with them, with some people that have some sense instead of those idiots in my grade."

"Well, if Emily's going."

"She's going."

"Please eat some supper."

"I can't eat supper. I can barely fit in my cheerleader skirt. Did you finish the black one? I have to have it. Is it done yet?"

"It's on the worktable. We'll try it on after dinner. I don't know why they want you to have black. I think it's very unflattering on young girls."

"It's just what they want." Rhoda kissed her mother on the cheek and went back to scrambling her egg. She scrambled it in several pats of butter. At the last minute she added an extra egg. If she didn't eat anything else until to-morrow night it would be all right. Already she could feel her rib cage coming out. She would be so beautiful. So thin. Surely he would love her.

"That's really all you're going to eat?"

"That's all. I ate a huge lunch." She dumped the scrambled eggs onto a plate and went out of the kitchen and through the living room and sat in the alcove of the stairs, with the phone sitting about three feet away. Soon it would be tomorrow. It would ring and his voice would be on the line and he would call her Cheetah and then he would be there and she would be in his arms and life would begin.

Then death will come, she remembered. Then you will die and be inside a coffin in a grave. Forever and ever and ever, world without end, amen. Rhoda shivered. It was true. Death was true. And she was included. She ate the eggs.

* * *

Then it was Friday, then Friday night. Then he was there, standing in her living room, with his wide brow and his wide smile and his terrible self-confidence, not the least bit bothered by her mother's lukewarm welcome or that her father didn't come out of the dining room to say hello. Then they were out the door and into his car and it was just as she had dreamed it would be. The quality of his skin when she touched his arm, the texture, was so pure, so white, even in the dark his skin was so white. He was sick and his body was fighting off the sickness and the sickness was in the texture of his skin but something else was there too. Power, will, something like his music was there, something going forward, driving, something that was not going to let him die. She wanted to ask him about the sickness, about Saint Louis, about the operations, but she did not dare. The forward thing, the music, would not allow it. Even Rhoda, as much as she always talked of everything, knew not to talk of that. So she was quiet, and kept her hand on his arm as he drove the car. She waited.

"I'm so goddamn proud of you," he said. "You're doing it. You're going to do it, just like I said you would."

"It's just because of you," she answered. "It's just to make you like me. Oh, hell, now I'm going to cry. I'm pretty sure I'm going to cry." He stopped the car on the side of the road and pulled her into his arms and began to kiss her. There was a part of her rib cage in the back that was still sort of fat but not too fat. If I was standing up I'd be skinny, she decided. It's not fair to kiss sitting down.

"You don't ever wait for anything, do you?" he said. "I had meant to make you wait for this." He handed it to her. Put it in her hand. The metal cut into her palm, the ruby in the center embedded in her palm. "You'll have to wear it on the inside of your bra. We aren't supposed to give them to children."

"I'm not a child. You know I'm not a child."

"Yeah, well Tau chapter of ZBT doesn't know anything except you're a freshman in high school. Don't get me thinking about it."

"Are you giving me this pin or not?"

"I'm giving it to you." He turned her around to face him. "I'm giving it to you because I'm in love with you." He laughed out loud, his wonderful laugh, the laugh he had been laughing the first time she laid eyes on him, when he was leaning up against the concrete block wall of the Coca-Cola bottling plant picking her out to be his protégée. "I'm in love with a girl who is fourteen years old."

"Say it again," she said. "Say you love me."

"After the ball game."

"No, right now. In front of Janet Allen's house. Right here, so I'll always remember where it was."

"I love you. In this Plymouth in front of Janet Allen's house." Then he kissed her some more. There were a lot of long crazy kisses. Then Rhoda pinned the ZBT pin to the inside of her bra and later, every time she jumped up to cheer at the ball game she could feel it scratch against her skin and send her heart rampaging all over the Benton football field and out across the hills and pastures of Little Egypt and down the state of Illinois to the river.

On Sunday he went back to school. Drove off down the street smiling and waving and left her standing on the sidewalk, by the nandina bushes. She walked down Bosworth Street to Cynthia's house and sat on the swing all afternoon telling Cynthia every single thing they had said and done

all weekend, every word and nuance and embrace, every
bite they ate at the drive-in and what kind of gas he bought
and how he cursed the gas tank and the story of his mother
cursing out the Lieutenant Governor of Illinois. When
Cynthia's mother called her to dinner, Rhoda walked back
home, trying to hold the day inside so it would never end.

There was a meatloaf for dinner and macaroni and
cheese and green peas and carrots and homemade rolls. All
her favorite dishes. After dinner her father called them into
the living room and told them the news. They were moving
away. He had bought them a white Victorian mansion in a
town called Franklin, Kentucky, and in a month they
would move there so he could be nearer to the mines. "It's
too far to drive," he said. "I can't make these drives with all
I have to do."

"We're going to move again?" Rhoda said. "You are
going to do this to me?"

"I'm not doing anything to you, Sister," he said. "You're
a little silly girl who's still wet behind the ears. I know
what's best for all of us and this is what we're going to do.
You're going to love it there."

"I'm going to have a play," she said. "I've just written
the Senior Play. I have written the Senior Play for the
whole school. They're going to put it on. Are you listening
to me?" No one else said a word. It was only Rhoda and her
father. Her mother was on the green chair with her arms
around Dudley. "I won't leave. I don't believe you'd do this
to me. You can't do this to me."

He lifted his chin. He stuck his hands in his pockets.
Their eyes met. "You do what I tell you to do, Miss Priss.
I'm the boss of this family."

"He can't do this to me." Rhoda turned to her mother. "You can't let him do this. You can't let it happen."

"I tried, my darling," her mother said. "I have told him a hundred times."

"I won't go," Rhoda said. "I'll stay here and live with Cynthia." Then she was out the door and running down the street and was gone a long time walking the streets of Harrisburg, Illinois, trying to believe there was something she could do.

Four weeks later the yellow moving van pulled up in front of the house on Rollston Street and the boxes and furniture and appliances were loaded on the van. Rhoda stayed down the street at Mike Ready's house talking and listening to the radio. She didn't feel like seeing her friends or telling them goodbye. She didn't tell anyone goodbye, not Dixie Lee or Shirley or Naomi, not even Letitia or Cynthia Jane. She just sat at Mike Ready's shuffling a deck of cards and talking about the basketball team. Around four o'clock she went home and helped her mother close the windows and sweep the debris on the floor into neat piles. "We can't leave a mess for the next people," her mother said. "I can't stand to move into a dirty house."

"Where's Dudley?" Rhoda asked. "Where's he gone?"

"He went with your father. They've gone on. You're going to drive with me. We need to finish here, Rhoda, and get on our way. It's going to be dark before too long. I want to drive as far as possible in the light."

"How long will it take?"

"About three hours. It isn't that far away. We can come back all the time, Rhoda. You can come back to see your play."

"I don't care about the goddamn play. Don't talk about the play. Let's get going. What else do we have to do?"

Then they were in the car and headed out of town. They drove down the main street, then turned onto Decatur and drove past the store where Anne Layne was working still, selling clothes to people off of racks, a frown on her face, caught forever in a world she could not imagine leaving for good reasons or bad ones, past the drugstore where Philip Holloman would sit every Saturday of his life on the same stool until it closed the year he was thirty-nine and he had to find a new place to hang out in on Saturdays. Past the icehouse and the filling station and the drive-in and past the brick fence of Bob Rosen's grandmother's house, where his gray Plymouth would come to rest. Past the site of the new consolidated school and the park where Rhoda had necked with Bob Rosen when he was still going steady with Anne Layne and past the sign that said City Limits, Harrisburg, Illinois, Population 12,480. Come Back Soon. You're Welcome.

It grew dark swiftly as it was the middle of December. December the fourteenth. At least it's not my lucky number, Rhoda thought, and feel asleep, her hand touching the edge of her mother's soft green wool skirt, the smell of her mother's expensive perfume all around them in the car. The sound of the wheels on the asphalt road. When she woke they were pulling onto the wide steel bridge that separates Illinois from Kentucky. Rhoda sat up in the seat. It was the Ohio River, dark and vast below her, and the sky was dark and vast above with only a few stars and they were really leaving.

"I don't believe it," she said. "I don't believe he'd do this to me." Then she began to weep. She wept terrible uncontrollable tears all across the bridge, weeping into her hands, and her mother wept with her but she kept her hands on the wheel and her eyes on the road. "There was nothing I could do about it, darling," she said. "I told him over and over but he wouldn't listen. He doesn't care about anything in the world but himself. I don't know what else I could have done. I'm so sorry. I know how you feel. I know what you are going through."

"No, you don't," Rhoda said, turning her rage against her mother. "You don't know. You could have stopped him. You don't know. You lived in the same house every day of your life. Your house is still there. Your mother is still there in that same house. You went to one school. You had the same friends. I don't care about this goddamn Franklin, Kentucky. I hope it burns to the ground. I won't like it. I hate it. I already hate it. Oh, my God. I hate its guts." Her mother took one hand from the wheel and touched her arm.

"Good will come of it, Rhoda. Good comes of everything."

"No, it doesn't," she said. "It does not. That's a lie. Half the stuff you tell me is a lie. You don't know what you're saying. You don't know a goddamn thing. STOP THIS GODDAMN CAR. I HAVE TO GO TO THE BATHROOM. STOP IT, MOTHER. I MEAN, STOP IT RIGHT THIS MINUTE. THE MINUTE YOU GET OFF THIS BRIDGE."

Ariane stopped the car and Rhoda strode off across a field and urinated behind a tree. The warm urine poured

out upon the ground and steam rose from it and that so-
laced her in some strange way and she pulled up her pants
and walked back across the stubble and got into the car.

"It better be a big house," she said. "It had better be the
biggest house in that goddamn town."

Adoration

I$_T$ $_{WAS}$ C$_{HRISTMAS}$ in Atlanta and Rhoda was sick every day. She was so sick she could hardly go to work. She would get better, then get worse. It couldn't have happened at a more inconvenient time because she had just been promoted to the Shopping Service at J. P. Allen's Department Store. She ran up and down the stairs in a red dress buying things for people to give to other people. She ran up and down and talked on the phone to rich ladies about their shopping problems.

She was nineteen years old and she had been married six months and she was putting her husband through school. She made four hundred dollars a month and his parents gave them four hundred more and her father gave her anything she asked him for.

She had made love to a boy one night after a fraternity

party. The next week they ran away and got married. A
month later she was living in a garage apartment in Atlanta putting him through school. Sex had been a big surprise to Rhoda. She had felt its mighty hand.

"What are you doing this for?" Her friend Daniel, who
was an artist, had stopped by the store to take her out to
lunch. "Why did you quit school?"

"I had to. I have to put him through college."

"You're crazy. Throwing yourself away."

"Of course I'm crazy, darling. Aren't we all?" She
laughed a wonderful sophisticated laugh. It was Rhoda's
main affectation when she was nineteen to say darling as
many times as possible every day. Her other obsession was
learning to dress like the salesladies at J. P. Allen's, especially a slim dark woman with a bun who wore black
leather heels trimmed in brass. Rhoda made four hundred
dollars a month and she charged about six hundred a
month to the store and her father was still coming out
ahead. Then she got sick and it all stopped.

She couldn't believe this terrible sickness, this bleeding
and bleeding and bleeding. She couldn't be pregnant because she almost always wore the diaphragm. She lay in
bed in the garage apartment and bled and bled and bled.
Her young husband sat on the edge of the bed and worried.
He thought he had wounded her. He was scared to death of
Rhoda's terrible blood. He wished he had never run off and
married her no matter how much money her father had. It
was terrible. She was a terrible cook and she followed him
around all the time and now all she did was bleed.

"Let me call my aunt Lillian. You'd better go to a doctor, Rhoda. You'd better find out what's wrong."

"I can't get up. Tell the doctor to come over here."

"They don't come out in Atlanta. Let me call my aunt."

"All right. Call her then." Rhoda lay back on the pillows. The room was dark, shrouded by the bamboo blinds she had installed in all the windows. The room was a mess, clothes were scattered everywhere. She was bleeding to death in a messy room.

"You've got an appointment this afternoon. They said to bring you in."

"I can't get up."

"Yes you can. I'll help you." Then he pulled her to the side of the bed and handed her some clothes and she put them on. Then he picked her up and carried her across the room and down the stairs and out the door. At least he's strong, Rhoda told herself. At least I had enough sense to marry someone strong.

They drove downtown and parked in a parking lot and went into a building and up an elevator and the nurse met them at the door and took them inside and put her on a table. "I'm bleeding all the time," Rhoda said. "I've been bleeding for days."

"We know," the nurse said. She put her hand on Rhoda's arm and Rhoda went to sleep. Maybe she went to sleep. She never could remember what happened next or when they told her. It always seemed she heard the news from deep within a dream. When she woke up she was in the back seat of the car. Her husband was driving her to Alabama to her mother. "What are we doing?" she said. "Where are we going? What's going on?"

"We're going to Decatur. You're going to have a baby. Rhoda, please lie down."

"Oh, my God. I don't believe it. Oh, I hope it's a boy. I want a boy." She fell into a dream. She was on Finley Island by the water. Her little boy was with her. He held onto her hand. She would teach him to swim. He would

swim the English Channel. He would dive from cliffs and
be a hero to end all heroes. She woke up because blood was
running down her legs again, over her skirt, her legs, the
car. "You have to stop and buy me some Kotex," she said.
"I have to have some new pajamas. I can't show up at
Momma's like this." They stopped at a store in a small
town on the Alabama line and she went in and bought
clean clothes and a pair of blue silk pajamas and a robe.
A musty-smelling lady in a bun helped her back into the
car. She lay down on the seat holding her packages and
when she woke again she was in the hospital and they
were all around her, her mother and her father and her
husband and Doctor Greer, her own doctor who was kin
to her.

"Am I going to have a baby?" she asked.

"I don't know. We'll wait and see."

"Am I or not? I want to know."

"I'm not sure if you still have it. In the morning we'll
know." They gave her a shot and she slept some more. She
slept for eighteen hours. In the morning they bathed her
and brought her food and Doctor Greer was alone with her,
his snow-white head was beside her bed, his hand was on
her hands. "I think we will have to go on and get rid of this
one, Rhoda. There will be plenty more." Good, Rhoda
thought, I didn't want to have a baby anyway. Then she
began to cry. Terrible tears. Doctor Greer patted her hand
and said, "This too shall pass away."

"I like it," she said. "I want it. I like it inside of me."

"All right," he said. "We'll wait another day." A nurse
appeared and gave her another shot and she went back to
sleep, back into the dream of the island and the water and
the boy. The boy was floating away. Come back, she

screamed. She tore out into the water, swimming her best Australian crawl. He drifted farther and farther away. Come back, Rhoda called, with her mouth half full of water. Come back. I want you. Come back to me. He floated on his back, so beautiful, so perfect, so new. He would not drag her down and drown her. He was her little boy. Her father appeared on the pier. "Catch him. Goddammit, Sister. Swim, show me what you're made of." A group of ladies were around her father, in their dresses and their heels and their perfume. They loved him and he loved them. He talked to them and listened when they spoke. He never pushed them away. Was never cold to them.

It was dark when Rhoda woke again. She thought she must have been asleep for hours. Everything was very dreamy in the room. The white curtains swayed on their stems, the silver utensils gleamed on the enamel table. A nurse with her hat awry was by her side. A needle was in her arm. Doctor Greer was so close she could smell his shaving cream. "How're we doing?" he said.

"I don't know. You tell me."

"I think it's all right, Rhoda. I think you'll keep the baby."

"Are you sure?"

"Not yet."

"Well, make up your mind. You tell me one thing and then you tell me another. Where's my husband?"

"He's here. He wants to see you." Her husband was in the doorway. He looked very handsome in his suit. He looked very sure of himself, like a grown man, tall and brave and wide. He took her hands. He kissed her very gently. "I hope it's true," he said.

"It will be a boy," Rhoda said. "I wouldn't have anything else."

They moved to the new apartment in January. Rhoda threw the last box on the bedroom floor and sank down on the bed. Her husband came into the room. The baby was asleep in his crib. He was two months old. He was perfect. He was so beautiful they looked at him all day. They looked at him so much they almost forgot to argue. They liked him so much they were almost happy.

"Don't do that," Rhoda said. "I'm out of jelly."

"We won't do anything. We'll just put it in."

"No."

"Come on."

"Okay."

"Let's make another one. They come out so nice. I want some more."

"You're crazy."

"Please."

"Okay."

"You're an angel."

"You are too."

It was an ecstatic pregnancy. Rhoda lived on diet pills and potato chips and gin. She lived on vegetable soup and cornbread and Cokes and gin. She went to the doctor every two weeks because he was the best-looking man in Atlanta. She went down one day in July and had the baby because it was coming too soon. They cut her open and took him out and sewed her back up and later that night she wrote her father a long letter. Some days later he wrote her back and sent her some money. Her mother came and stayed and took care of her and got her a new maid and bought her some books to read. It was a good month to have a baby. There was a new book by Ernest Hemingway on the shelves. *Across the River and into the Trees.* It was a wonderful book about the excitement and romance of love in Venice between a young countess and an old army colonel who was about to die. Thank God for books, Rhoda was thinking. Since nothing ever happens around here.

It was dark in the house. A dark house at the end of a curved street on a hill in Kansas City, Kansas. It was two o'clock in the morning and it was Rhoda's birthday. She had been twenty-six years old for two drunken hours and she woke up in the dark and felt for her husband and began to laugh at something they had done at a bar. Drunk, drunk, drunk. They had been drunk since six o'clock the night before and they hadn't even had a fight yet. "Make love to me," she said. "I mean it. Do it now."

"Go put on your diaphragm."

"I don't want to. Use a rubber."

"Oh, shit, that's no good."

"It will do." She reached in a drawer beside the bed and got one out that had been there for ages. They began to giggle, laughing and making love because it felt good and was fun. In a while it became apparent that the rubber was not doing a bit of good. "Go take a douche."

"Oh, shit, I'm too tired to move."

"Go on."

"All right." She climbed out of bed and went into the bathroom and turned on the light and stood against the doorframe giggling some more. She was wearing a white silk nightgown with blue embroidery on the top and she was making a baby right that very minute and she knew it and she didn't give a damn because it was her birthday and she thought it was funny. He would be a laughing baby who would love music and have a thousand freckles. I might as well go on and have him and get it over with, Rhoda decided. I might as well go on and get him here. She put her head against the doorframe and saw his face smiling up at her and she thought it was just as funny as it could be and she adored it and she sat down on the floor and laughed some more.

"What are you laughing at?" the father of Rhoda's babies said to her. "What's all that goddamn laughing?"

"It's just funny, that's all. It's hilarious."

"Are you going to take a douche?"

"No, it's too much trouble."

"Then get back in bed."

"I will in a minute."

"We have to stop drinking so much. We have to save some money."

"I know. I think we should. I'm going to start tomorrow."

She climbed back into bed and cuddled up in her husband's arms. This one will be the swimmer, she decided. This is the one who will swim the channel for me.

II
Bad Times in
a Good Land

The Emancipator

MAE LAUER-CHEENE came home from the Peace Corps to
a city that seemed to float above the prairies, a city that
wanted to do good, had done good, was going to keep on
doing good. I can settle down for good, she thought, I have
seen all of the world I need to see.

She was twenty-nine. It seemed a long journey had
brought her back to where she started from. She lugged her
suitcase up onto her father's porch. Her mother stood in the
doorway, a big woman with soft features and cool hands.
"We've waited so long to see you," she said. "We're so glad
you're back." Then they were all in the kitchen, her brother
too, the four of them, just as it had been all the years of her
growing up.

"What are they like over there?" her brother said. He
was wearing a T-shirt from a Police concert. It seemed too

small for his big German stodginess, too silly to sit upon
such a chest. He folded his hands across it as if he were
reading her mind. He hid his silliness beneath his hands.

"It is so poor. You cannot imagine. Nothing I say can
make you believe how many there are. They are starving.
Children too. At first I could not sleep. For a long time I
couldn't sleep."

"They have too many babies," her father said. "They
breed like fleas."

"We send them wheat," her mother said. "We send half
our food over there."

"I didn't mean it was our fault,'" Mae said. "This pie is
wonderful. I knew you'd have it for me."

"They've been calling you every day," her father said.
"About counseling the foreign students. I guess you've got
the job. They called twice one day."

"Oh, that's good. Who called? Did the dean call?" She
stood up, remembering who she was, her credentials, her
languages, her degrees.

"I fixed up your room," her mother said. "You're going
to stay here awhile, aren't you?"

"Of course I am. I've been lonely for you. I want to sleep
in your sheets, be your little girl." She giggled. Her parents
smiled into each other's eyes. Her brother joined their pleasure. Mae stood above them, her lovely big body, her long
arms, her bright light-colored hair. Long bones, long undulations, the best of her kind, a beautiful German girl.

He was Lebanese. The third student she saw the first
day. His English was like a child's, careful and full of sur-
prises. "You've had so much trouble," she said. "Your

home has been such a battlefield. I am in sympathy with
that. I want you to know that about me."

"You are too kind. It is enough I take your time with
these problems."

"What is wrong? What can we do?" She looked into his
face. Alone in a foreign country. She could empathize with
that, the loneliness, the courage. His shirt was a soft peach
color, carefully ironed, pleated beige slacks, hard strong
arms. It had been a month since she left the married
Englishman standing on the platform in Delhi. She had
been glad to leave him, glad to go away from secrecy and
pain. She was ready for another chance, this time it would
be better. She was sure of that. Love doesn't have to be sorrow, she told herself. Surely there is love without sorrow. If
she could conceive of it, wouldn't it be possible to find it? If
she was good enough? If she deserved it by her work, her
kindness, her humanity. Surely it was there, a simple place
where men and women could lie down in joy and rise up in
joy.

"What can we do to help?" she said again. "How can I
be of service?"

"It is my visa. It is running out. I think they have made a
mistake. Here, these are the papers. What do you think?
Can you understand this?" He put a folder down on her
desk, his visa, a letter of introduction to the president of the
university, several other pieces of correspondence. The visa
would run out in a month. He had been denied an extension.

"Why didn't they give you an extension?"

"I do not know. They will not tell me. I have not caused
trouble. However, I did attend a meeting on the campus

and wore a badge they gave me. It was for the problem of voting in student elections. I was for the ones that said yes."

"Let me keep these for a few days," she said. "I'm new at this job. I'll have to find out what channels to go through. Are you enrolled now, this semester?"

"Oh, yes, I have paid my tuition for the whole summer. I paid in advance."

"Please come back in a few days," she said. "Your visa will be safe. I'll lock it in my drawer."

"You are too kind to me. I am grateful to you for your time." He stood up. She stood up behind her desk. He bent over her hand. A diplomat's gesture. "I will come each day to see you," he said. He put his lips against her knuckles. His mouth breathed on her fingers. He kept his mouth there for a long time. Her hand was moist when he gave it back. His breath was between her fingers like a web on summer grass. She could almost see it there. Oh, no, she thought. This shouldn't happen.

When he was gone she sat down in the chair and let her hands wander into her lap. Un, huh. She giggled. A black girl she had roomed with in Delhi had taught her the expression. Why not, she decided. I'm alive, I can't help that. I'm glad I'm still alive. After that sea of starving babies it's a wonder I can feel a thing. Those eyes, a girl could drown in that man's eyes.

His name was Hadi Karami Deeb. He was from northern Lebanon, from a Sunni family of renegade Muslims. For twenty generations his family had lived in a mountainous village called Hadchite, on a rock outthrust extending right into the gorge of the Kadishi Valley. The precipice in the village was a constant danger. Every few years a villager "forgot himself" and walked "out of the village" and was killed. Hadi had grown up beside that precipice, a land of steep slopes and escarpments, boulders and stones, the wind whistling between the rocks, the river pounding through the canyon. "Be careful," someone was always saying to him. "Take care."

When he was twelve his father had taken his wife and children and left the village to set up shop in Tripoli, selling goods the villagers made from their sheep, parchment and yarn and rugs. The shop prospered. Hadi's father dreamed of the future. He sent his sons to English schools. He applied for scholarships for them. Hadi's applications were successful. When he was twenty-one he was flown to the state of Nebraska to attend business school. He had been there almost two years when he met Mae. "Find a German girl," his friends had told him. "They are like little machines. They are blond and they work hard. Make one love you and you will never have to go home."

But how was he to make one of those goddesses love him? No matter how polite he was, or how well dressed, no matter how many careful advances he made, they turned away. Their great blond beauty found him wanting. "One will come along," his friends consoled him. "They get lonely like all women. They become weak. You must watch for it. You will know the one."

He was at Mae's office at ten the next morning. She was wearing a white skirt, a purple and white striped blouse, her best gold bracelets, sandals. "Come in and talk awhile," she said. "I haven't been able to get anyone to tell me what to do but I'll make some calls if you don't mind waiting. I need your records from the administration building. Could you get them for me?"

"Of course," he said. "Whatever I can do to help." She picked up the phone and asked someone to release the papers to him. "It's room two twenty-two on the second floor." She paused, then went on. "We could have lunch together, if you like. I like to talk to people from other places, hear their stories."

"I would like that," he said. "I will take you to a nice place I found out about."

She busied herself while he was gone. Called the passport bureau. Talked to her boss. "There was some sort of trouble, a group of Muslim students," he said. "It was a problem in the community. If he was involved you're out of luck, Mae. They don't fool around with the ones from the Middle East. It's touchy around here."

"That's unbelievably limited. It isn't fair. He's paid a whole summer's tuition."

"You weren't here. There was a lot in the papers. It was a real stink. Well, call over at the governor's office. See if Jane Reed can help. See what you get over there."

She sighed. She straightened her shoulders and breathed into the place the Indians call the anahata. A wide heart, she thought. I have a wide heart. I have escaped the archetype.

They went to a restaurant called The Red Onion. He held the door open for her. As she moved past his arm she could smell the strange perfume of his skin. Their eyes met. Her smile caressed his foreignness, she surrounded him with her smile. A memory of being alone in Stockholm one winter, brutally homesick and disoriented, came to her. She placed her hand on his arm. "This is so nice," she said. "How nice of you to bring me here. I didn't know they had this. It's new since I was gone." A maître d' appeared and showed them to a table in an alcove near the bar. There was a skylight above the table. Rain was beginning to fall. The skylight was shaped like a kite. Stained glass and skylights were everywhere, jazz was playing.

"That's John Coltrane," she said. "A great composer. He didn't write it down. But he recorded it and taught it to people and so we have it. Do you like jazz?"

"Oh, yes. I want to learn such things. You will teach me about your music, yes?" She giggled. She ordered a martini, then another. He told her women in his country did not drink. They laughed at that. He told her how frightened he was, how he feared going home. He lit her cigarettes with great courtesy. She cupped her hands around the matches he proffered her. He talked lightly of political plots, jail cells, torture, the realities of the world he had left. He spread his hands out on the table. "I am frightened of going back. It did not occur to me they would not let me stay."

"I'll fix it," she said. "I'll think of something. Why didn't you come to the Center before? You shouldn't have been dealing with this all alone. I can imagine how confusing it's been."

"I came there once. The lady said they would call me back but they never did. Perhaps they lost my number. I didn't want to keep bothering them." He tossed his head. A proud man. Mae reached over and covered his hand with hers. He lifted her hand to his mouth. He kissed her palm. He left his lips on her palm for a long time.

"I like to walk in the afternoons," she said. "I'll take you walking around Lincoln and show you where you are."

"When can we do that?" He was still holding her hand.

"This afternoon if you like. I'll take you to the park. There are buffaloes in the park. Real buffaloes. I'll show them to you." He lifted her hand back up to his mouth.

There was no one in the world but Mae and Hadi. "I want you to stop worrying about this visa mess," she added. "That's just asinine red tape. We'll fix that up."

His appeal took a while to be processed. In the meantime Mae began to spend the evenings at his apartment in the bed-and-breakfast house where he worked part time as a waiter. A small old-fashioned bedroom with high windows. A double mattress on the floor. A shelf of books in Arabic and English and French. A poster from a museum, a photograph of his parents and his brothers.

The late sun fell across the bed. His fingers wove into her muscles. He sang to her. "Such beauty, such a beauty, a goddess thrown down upon my bed. Praise be to Allah, who gives all good things, a flower, a goddess, a singing bird, a tree."

"My father was the eldest son," he told her. "He was taught to read. For this reason he could go to Tripoli and have a better life. In Hadchite there is nothing. But men in Hadchite are free. They are unpopular with the government because they do not do as they are told. No one minds in Hadchite even if you beat them and take their flour away. So my family is in trouble with the government. My father writes me not to come back there. He must be careful what he writes. Only I can understand the things he says to me in his letters." He paused. "You cannot imagine this. This is only a story to you." He moved his body beside hers, caressing her with his hands. He lifted her hand to his mouth. He ran his tongue down into the spaces between her fingers.

"What would happen if you go back?"
"They would arrest me when I got off the plane. They

would take me off. I don't know after that. Perhaps they
would offer me work now that I am educated. I think
they would kill me. They do not trust men with my name.
When will the papers come back?"

"I'll call all the places again tomorrow. I'll do something.
I'll call the governor again. He's a good man. His leg was
shot off in the war. He will help us."

"Once there was a shepherd," he told her, moving his
arm to cushion her head. "And he wished to make a poem
for his beloved. He took a kid and killed it and cut the skin
from its stomach and boiled it in lye and let it sit for many
days, changing the water each day. He stretched the skin
on a frame made of willow, drawing the strings tighter and
tighter until the skin was the color of sand. He trapped a
raven and took a feather from its right wing and dipped it
in the jucie of wild berries and held it above the skin. No
words came. He walked down to the river and listened to its
song. He returned to the skin and took up the pen. Once
there was a shepard, he wrote, who wished to make a poem
for his beloved. . . ."

The application was turned down. "They can't send him
home." Mae stormed around her boss's office. "This is the
United States. There was no arrest, no conviction. He has
done nothing. What can I do? Who can I see?"

"This is a federal matter, Mae." Her boss hung his big
Danish head. He was a level-headed civilized man. He believed in law, in categories and realms of discourse. "This is
not a Nebraska matter. You have to go to the federal
building and work it out over there. You'll have to call
someone in Washington."

"It was just a bunch of students wanting to vote in the
goddamn student elections. It wasn't worth a hill of beans.

It wasn't even violent. All it was was a bunch of signs. What's going on around here?"

"Call someone in our delegation in Washington. Try Ned Sandoz. See if anyone in his office can lend a hand."

Mae spent several weeks on the phone and in correspondence with federal bureaus while the days of Hadi's visa ran out. "We will have to part," he said. "This is the saddest thing of all for me. I have never known such happiness. Now I will only remember it." He lifted her palm to his cheek. She felt the breath move in and out of his nostrils, the wonder of his jaw, the wonder of his neck.

"There will be something to do," she said. "We have another week. We'll think of something. I won't let you leave. I won't let you go back there."

So she married him. In her mother's parlor with a Lutheran minister and her mother and father and brother and a cousin for a bridesmaid and two waiters from his bed-and-breakfast place and the next-door neighbors. Afterwards there was coffee and strudel and wedding cakes that looked like mounds of snow. Everyone ate the cakes and talked very excitedly for a while, then Mae and Hadi made their escape in her Opel. They drove to the little house they had rented on Vincent Street. They walked into the living room. They stretched out their hands to each other. Mae reached up and undid a button on her blouse.

"We are here," she said. "This is our home."

"You are my wife now."

"Yes, I am."

"We will have happiness. We will have a good time."

"Yes. We will."

*   *   *

He taught her to make coffee the way he was accustomed to it. They laughed and joked as he showed her how the beans must be ground just so and the water poured a thimbleful at a time and how the consistency could be judged by putting a drop in the palm. How the liquid would ball up in her palm if it was strong enough. He showed her three times.

The fourth morning she rushed through the process, pulling on her clothes as she fixed his eggs and toast, watching the clock. He lifted the cup and tasted the coffee and walked over and spat it out into the sink. He turned to her. She giggled and started to speak. He hit her across the face. "It is too thin," he said. "It tastes like goat urine." He went into the spare room and closed the door behind him. When she returned in the afternoon he was not there. Nothing had been touched. The house was exactly as she had left it. The coffee cup with the remains of the coffee sat on the edge of the sink. She walked through the house, then sat down on the front steps and lit a cigarette. The sun was still high. It would be several hours before it went down.

In two days he returned, wearing a new white shirt. "I have been thinking of you," he said.

"Are you going to apologize?" she said. "Because it's going to take more than that."

"I do not know why I have done this to you," he said. "I am going back to Lebanon. I will go this afternoon to buy my ticket." He stood before her. She saw them leading him into the interrogation room, saw them surround him, the thumbscrews, the whips come out.

"Oh, no," she said. "Don't do that. Anyone can make a mistake. Come with me. Come lie down." They went together to the bed. His fingers found her fingers. His mouth covered her neck with kisses. He brought her fruit and cheese cut up on a plate, wine in a china cup. He put pieces into her mouth and sang as he made love to her, strange involved melodies. She slept a long time afterwards. They were far away from anything either of them had ever known. She had not been this far away in India. He had not been this far away when his plane landed in San Francisco, and on that day he had thought he was on the moon.

In May she took him to a party at the museum. The governor was there with his girlfriend. His girlfriend leaned on his arm, looking like a nymph in a white dress, and it seemed to Mae that the whole state of Nebraska must be in love. Nebraska had found its destiny. It would lead the world in love.

One of the governor's assistants was an old school friend of Mae's. He engaged her in a conversation about her work in India. Hadi stood off to one side watching his wife in the shadow of another man, her breasts shaking when she laughed, her uncovered arms and legs and neck.

A white-coated waiter appeared at his elbow carrying a tray of glasses. "Champagne?" he said.

"Thank you," Hadi said. He lifted a glass from the tray. He drank from it. He saw a reflection of himself in the glass wall of the museum. He saw himself and the waiter and the governor and the governor's girlfriend and Mae's friend and Mae. He saw the reflection of a female nude sitting with her bronze legs pulled up against her bronze chest. Her bronze vulva caught the light. He saw the village of Hadchite coming into the room, filing in through the glass wall, his mother and father and sisters and Mari and Khe and Bekaa and Mariam and Yusef and Shukrallah and

Zaiden and Nassim. He shook off the vision. He looked around him. He could have fit the whole village into this museum, with room to stable the goats and pigs.

"I would like to go now," he said to Mae, interrupting her conversation with her friend. "It is time for us to go to our home."

"Of course," she said. "All right."

They went out of the museum into the clear cool night. She reached out her hand to him. She allowed herself to be pulled along. His hand was tight and cold.

"Why did you fawn on that man so?" he said when they were home. He was taking off his rented tuxedo. He took off the cuff links. Pulled the studs out of the shirt. Undid the suspenders. "Why did you act like a whore to him?"

"To whom? To whom did I act like a whore? You've got to be kidding." She had her back to him, she was bending over to take off her shoes. He took hold of her arm. He turned her around. He hit her in the face with his fist.

When she woke up daylight was flooding the room. She pulled herself to the phone. She called the hospital. She didn't call her mother or her father or her brother because they had gone to Omaha to see her uncle.

He came to see her. He sat at the foot of her hospital bed and cried like a baby. He told her his terrible dreams. A dog that caught on fire from his breath. A girl caught in a fish net. A shepherd who came and grazed sheep on his land. "I am so frightened," he said. "I feel so alone. I will be better. I will be good to you. You will see. Or I will kill myself. I will save the world the trouble."

* * *

She relented. She allowed him to take her home. She set her mind in a straight line. She got up in the mornings and made the coffee exactly as he liked it. She ironed the clothes. She made up the bed. She allowed him to drive her to work in the mornings and pick her up in the afternoons. She was good. She was so good there would never be any reason to hurt her as long as she lived.

"What's wrong with you?" her boss said. "You look like hell. Are you pregnant? Do you think you're pregnant?"

"I quit wearing makeup," she said. "Why should a married woman wear makeup?"

Since she was good, because she was good, Hadi would sit on the floor and look up at her with his wide eyes. He would put her fingers one by one into his mouth. His tongue would find her fingers, move down into her palm. Kiss, kiss, kiss. Go into the bed and wait for me, he would say. I will come in to you when I am ready. She would do as she was told. A long time would go by. Then he would come to her.

"I don't like what's going on over here," her mother said. "I don't like the feel of it." She was sitting on the stiff brown sofa in the living room of Mae's house. Her purse was in her lap. She was uncomfortable. She was not in the habit of telling her children what to do. "Your father thinks you look bad."

"We're fine, mother. He only has a few more courses to take. Another semester. Then we'll both have jobs. There'll be more money."

"How did you do that to your arm? I never knew you to fall."

"I was standing on a chair and it broke. I told you that. I

was fixing things." She leaned back in the armchair. She looked away.

"I don't believe you. He hit you, didn't he? I think he hits you. Your father thinks so too. Why don't you ever come over? You haven't seen your brother since Thanksgiving."

"Are you warm enough in here? I can turn up the heat."

"Tell me what's going on, Mae. I told your father I'd come over here and see what's going on."

"We had some fights. I'll admit that. He's terrified, Mother. You've never been in a foreign country. You can't imagine what it's like, how isolated you feel. And he can't go home. That's closed to him."

"Thank God for that. Thank God you won't be going over there." She paused. It was a lot for her to say. "I don't know how you got into this. We shouldn't have let you go to India. That's how it began." She stood up. "'Will you come for dinner Sunday? Will you go to church with us on Sunday? There's going to be some music from the university. He could come."

"I might. I'll see. He has exams to study for."

"Couldn't you come without him? You could see your brother."

"I'll see. I'll see what I can do." It was quiet in the room. Mae relented. "I'll come," she said. "I'll come for sure. You pick me up, then." She moved across the room and sat down by her mother. She touched the soft flesh of her mother's arm. She put her chin down into her mother's side. Her mother patted her on the head, a quick nervous pat, not quite an embrace. A cold woman, Mae thought, a cold race. Ugly and cold, we have nothing to give but cold gifts. If I go back to them I will be like this, an old blond woman without feeling, with nothing to give but order and repetition and soft hanging blond flesh. An ugly boring race.

"Bring him too. We'll have dinner afterwards. I'll cook things he likes. What does he like?"

"Whatever you cook will be fine."

He was having trouble at the business school. He believed the dean's assistant had it in for him. She was the one who did degree checks. Students had to pass everything through her. Every time Hadi brought a schedule into her for approval she made him wait a long time.

"You can't finish without another accounting course," she was saying. "I'm sorry. I'm tired of talking to you about it. You can't get the degree without the requirements. I don't know who you think you are, Hadi."

"You must let me take this instead. I have no way to take them both at once. How can you expect me to take all this at once? It is because the classes are offered at the wrong time. Why don't you like me? What did I do to you?"

"Look here, don't start that with me." She stood up behind her desk, a small intense woman who published poetry in literary magazines. She met his eyes. "I'm not going to waste any more time on this. Don't come in here anymore until you get it straightened out. There are other people waiting to see me."

"I want to talk to the dean about this. I paid good money to get in here. I paid eighteen hundred dollars this year . . ."

She tightened her mouth. Goddamn rodents, she was thinking. Eric's right, we ought to let the Jews blow them off the face of the earth. "Get out of my office," she said. "Before I kick you out."

He left his jacket. After he was gone she picked it up. It

was a beige windbreaker from Miller-Paine. At least a hundred dollars' worth. Those goddamn Arabs, she thought. I'm going to quit this job if I have to keep putting up with this. She picked up her phone and got her boss. "Come take me for coffee," she said. "Come on, right now. I've got to talk."

She looked up. Hadi was back in the doorway. "If you would look at the things I brought. If you would give me credit for the courses I took in Beirut.'"

"Those papers don't mean anything over here. They aren't even in English. My accreditation standards won't allow me to honor those. No one told you you could bring those credits here. Now leave me alone, Hadi. I mean it. Get out of here." She looked right at him. A woman like a wall.

He walked out of the administration building and down the cobbled sidewalks between the yellow lilies and purple lithium and red salvia. A student gardener was kneeling over a sprinkler. She was wearing a pair of running shorts and a tank top. Her legs were folded under her. She squatted on her heels trying to adjust the water valve. "Tom, come look at this goddamn thing," she called to a boy who was working in the lilies. "Shit, if they don't get us some new equipment I'm quitting. Did you call them?" The water came on as she spoke, spewing out in Hadi's direction. "Well, shit," she said to him. "Didn't you see the sign? You're supposed to use the other walk in the afternoon."

Hadi raised his head, then backed away. "I'm sorry. I didn't see it."

"Well, read signs," she said, then turned back to her fellow worker. "Never mind, it's on now."

Hadi retraced his steps to the front of the administration building. He brushed the water from his trousers. He shifted his briefcase to his other arm and walked on down the street and crossed at the light and turned a corner and found his way to the Zoo Bar. Mae had asked him to meet her there at five. "Just this once," she said. "We never go anywhere. We never have any fun. I have to have some fun. These kids I went to school with are here. They're in Colorado now. They're only going to be here a few days."

"All right. I will go. I want to meet your friends."

"They're great people. They run a rafting business on the Colorado. Maybe they'll invite us out to go down it. You're always saying you're homesick for the mountains."

Hadi paused in the doorway of the dark-smelling place. Two boys were sitting at the bar watching television and drinking beer. A girl in a pink dress was playing a video machine. Hadi walked past them.

He saw Mae at a table past the bar. She was leaning with her elbows on the table, looking at a big redheaded man. They were laughing. Another man was leaning on a chairback, holding a stein of beer. A pitcher was on the table. Hadi backed up. The bartender picked up a glass and wiped it dry, then set it down on a counter, then came over. "Yes."

"Could I have a glass of water please? I've been walking in the sun."

"A what?"

"A glass of water."

"Teddy, get this guy a glass of water, would you?" The bartender called down the bar to his helper. "He wants a water." Hadi waited. In a few minutes the second man walked down his way and filled a glass from a hose and stuck it in front of him. "Here's your water."

"Thank you," Hadi said. He took the glass and walked on back to where Mae was. She was standing now, with her hand on the man's shoulder, listening to something he was telling her.

"So, this guy says, 'Darlene, put that life vest on or you can just sit here on this rock,' and she takes it and fucking knocks him out of the boat with it. She's from New Jersey or somewhere and she forgets about the buckle. So she just gets him right in the head with the buckle, and there I am, with twelve people paid and waiting to go down a river and I've got this guy on my hands out cold in the water."

"Hello," Hadi said, coming up, standing a few feet back. "I'm here."

"Oh, Dooley, here's my husband," she said. "This is Hadi. Hadi, these are my friends. Rick Ossian and this is Dooley. Oh, God, they've been telling me the funniest stories. Here, you want a beer?" Mae was drunk. She had left work early. She had been drinking beer since four. She smiled crazily in Hadi's direction. "Well, I can't believe you married this wild woman," Dooley said. "I couldn't ever get her to sit still long enough to fall in love with me. Hey," he took a drink of his beer and started laughing. "Did she ever learn to dance? I never could get her to dance. She'd step all over my feet. We used to try it with my sister, Judy. We'd tear up my mother's rugs trying to teach Mae to dance."

"She dances okay," he said. "She dances fine." He held his glass of water. A hadith was playing in his ear. If your enemy mocks you, do you exist? If your demon lives can you be said to live?

"We will be going now," he said. "It is time to make the evening meal."

"Oh, not now," she said. "It's Friday. We'll eat later. I want to finish talking to Dooley."

"Just one more beer," Dooley said. "I've got to go too, Mae. I promised Mother I'd be there for supper. I've got to run in a minute."

"Well, what a bunch of party-poopers. Look, what are you going to do later? You want to come back and hear the reggae? Let's keep the party going."

"Sure," Dooley said. "We'll come meet you. What time?"

"We can't come back this afternoon," Hadi said. "I have too much studies to do. Perhaps another time."

"Sure we can," Mae said. She finished off her beer. "I'm having a celebration. I'll be back," she added, speaking to Dooley, not looking in Hadi's direction. "I'll get here about eight-thirty and get us a table. It gets crowded when there's a band." Hadi moved over to her chair and pulled her up very gently from the table. "Let go of me," she said. "I can get up by myself."

Then, seeing his face, not wanting to argue in front of her friends, she let him lead her out between the tables and past the bar to the sidewalk. "Jesus," she said, turning to him, rising up on her heels until she was as tall as he was. "I'm sick of this, Hadi. I'm sick of being good. I'm a human being. I've got to have some fun now and then. I work hard all day. I'm a hard worker."

He didn't reply. He stuck his hands down into his pockets and walked without speaking to the car. Your women rise up and mock you. Your enemy lives and the enemy of your hara. Your demon and the demon of your father.

They rode down Vincent Street. It was very still. A hot still afternoon. Clouds were moving in, covering the sky. Hadi pulled to a stop before their house. Old Mr. Dierken and his wife were sitting on their porch. Hadi waved and they waved back. Mae got out and strode up the stairs. She went in and dropped her purse on the couch and started taking off her shoes. She had forgotten about being good. She was bored with her experiment in goodness.

"I don't know why you don't want to have any fun," she said. She took off her shoes and kicked them into a corner. "I'm working my ass off five days a week at that job. You told me you were going to get a part-time job to help out if your check didn't come. I've got bills piled up and Mother can't give me any more money because she's got William's tuition to pay." She faced him. She felt great. She was saying everything she'd been saving up. "I'm not taking this anymore, Hadi. There're going to be some changes around here."

Hadi walked toward her. There was nothing in his face to put her on her guard. "And I'll tell you something else," she began. He hit her in the solar plexus. Then hit her again. She flailed out at him with her arms. He hit her a third time, this time very hard. She doubled over onto the sofa. He reached beside her and pulled the belt out of an aquamarine polyester bathrobe she had thrown down that morning. He pulled her up by the hair. He wrapped the belt around her neck. Her hands flew up. He pushed her down onto the sofa and began to tighten the belt. It felt wonderful. It was wonderful to tighten the belt around her neck, to watch her eyes pop out.

Mae looked up into his face. "Oh, no," she rasped. "Oh, no, don't do it to me." Her hands came up again, then fell away. There was nothing now, no breath, nothing, only Hadi's veins and hands and eyes. His skin, his hands, his hair, teeth, nostrils, eyebrows, eyes.

He allowed her body to fall to the floor. He dropped the aquamarine cord beside it. He walked over to the sink and filled a glass with water and drank it. It was a glass from a pizza place. There was a picture of a little dwarf king with his crown askew. Little King, it said. He filled the glass again and drank from it.

He walked across the room and picked up the phone and called a friend, a fellow Lebanese student.

He took the car keys off the counter and walked out the door. He went back in and loosened a screen in the bed-room window. He rumpled up the covers on the bed, threw some clothes out of a dresser drawer. Then he left the house and drove over to his friend's apartment, a brick building on a side street near the capitol. He parked beside a red truck. He went in the building. There were some black people in the hallway, laughing and joking, waiting their turn at the washing machines. Their music was playing on a radio. Hadi drew in his breath. He hated their fat loose music, their fat loose ways. He knocked on his friend's door. When it was opened he went in. "Please fix me coffee," he said. "Could we play cards awhile?" The friend agreed. He put water on to boil and set up a small table and got out the dice and the cards. He fixed a tray of chocolates and brandied fruit and offered it to his guest. They talked in low voices of their past, of politics, which they vaguely un-derstood, of heroes and villians, of men they had never known who had created the destiny they found themselves in. "How is the German?" the host asked several times.

"She is very good to me," Hadi replied. "She has to have

me. She follows me around." He lowered his eyes as he said it. His host laughed. They laughed together.

I will play cards, Hadi said to himself. I will throw the dice. I will eat and drink. Time will pass. I will return to the house and find the body. I will run out into the street, tearing my shirt, beating my breast.

"You will come home with me later," he told his friend. "You will have dinner with me. The German will serve you lamb. You will see how she minds me." Hadi picked up the cards he had been dealt and studied them. A queen, a jack, a deuce, a pair of threes. Very good. One to discard. Lucky cards. A good and lucky day. A man takes what is dealt. He makes a life of it. So be it. It is ordered. It is planned. It is good.

Memphis

HER HORROR and fascination with his size. His power, his hands, feet, mouth, dick, all that stuff that carried her across the door of that little frame house on T Street and kept her there until her neck snapped. That's part of it. I have to tell you that part so you'll believe she stayed. I can't believe it and I was there. Katherine Louise Wheeler, Baby Kate, my niece, the daughter of a famous author and a Delta beauty. Cat, Franke called her, and Baby, Baby, all the time when they were doing it. They were always doing it.

"Wait till you meet him," she said. "And you will understand."

"All right. Bring him by."

"Wait till you see his shoulders. Three people could hide

behind his shoulders. His people cleared this land. We owe them their share."

"When's he coming?" I folded my hands in my lap. I stretched my mind. I am the family intellectual. I am supposed to be able to see beyond my fears. Then he was there. Coal black, powerful, full of laughter. I pictured the children. Light brown with that soft dusty cloudlike hair the children have when black men and blondes breed together. You've seen it. As if a wash of Clorox had been poured across a pickaninny. Pickaninny, what kind of a word is that? Will I never learn? Will it never end?

"How are you?" I said. "Baby Kate told me all about you."

"What did she say? What does she know to tell?" He took my hand. It slid into his like a trout returning to water. I decided he was a nice man. I was sure he was the nicest black man she could have found. "You fix apartments? She said you do it all alone. Make the plans and all."

"Could I have a drink of water? I've been in the sun all morning. I was playing tennis with some people from the mayor's office."

I went to get the water. When I returned she was sitting in his lap. "I have to get on to school," I said. "I have to give tests today. I wish I never had to give them. It hurts me more than it hurts them, that's what I always say."

"It's nice of you to let us use your place, Miss Wheeler. It's really nice of you."

"Thank you, Aunt Allie," she said, her eyes as solemn as an owl's. She walked me to the door. "He has to work tonight. You and I'll cook dinner together. I'll go shopping." She kissed me. I could smell her perfume. What was

I doing in this? I am fifty-four years old. I'm as crazy as a loon.

So first they were doing it in my apartment. The musk from those encounters rose up and invaded the walls. Hours after he was gone I could feel his breath on everything.

I am only a few blocks from the Memphis State campus where I teach. I walked home slowly all that summer. I would stop and inspect trees, read the memorial plaques on benches. Class of 1903. Veterans of World War II, In Memory of Carmen Carson Garth, Class of 1915. Site of the First Earth Science Class, 1923.

It was hot that summer. Hot and dry. The rain stayed over the Ozarks and made us dry. At night the jasmine and catalpa and honeysuckle turned the town into a bordello. The students walked the streets in twos and threes and licked ice cream cones and hardly seemed to speak and by the twenty-ninth of June my office desk was littered with pathetic little notes and scraps of paper. Miss W, can you forgive me? Miss Wheeler, can I see you after class to explain where I have been? Professor Wheeler, you won't believe the mess I'm in. I am so sorry I couldn't come yesterday. If you could wait till Friday for the paper . . . and so on. Fine, I told them. Sure. Of course, I understand.

I turned my office radio on to WKSS, Nothing But Love Songs, and thought about them doing it on my bed.

He came from West Memphis in a rented white Chevrolet and found her on the university track and told her he was a real estate developer. She believed him. She had done it with him a dozen times before she noticed the scars on his neck or finally got stoned or drunk enough to ask for details. He told her the truth. I'll say that for him. He never told any of us a lie. And it was true he knew the mayor.

His name was Franke Brown and his father was a janitor and his mother collected welfare and Baby Kate thought she had finally found a way to get her father to notice her, to acknowledge she was here. Her father, my brother, Hailey Wheeler. He wrote all those books about man's inhumanity to man. He sat on Big Hodding's right hand when they integrated the Delta schools. He knew Walker Percy and Shelby Foote and all the big ones. He had been the hit of a thousand New York cocktail parties, telling anyone who would listen about where he stood and what it has cost him in family and friends and inheritance and now here he was confronted with Baby Kate doing it with the biggest black man who had ever stood as a guest in our entrance hall. Well, he lost it, as the children say. The whole pack of cards came down.

"Get out," he told her. "How dare you bring that trash into my house." He let her take her clothes. Whatever she could fit into her car.

She came to me. What's an old maid for but to take in the strays? "He can't live here too," I told her. "The place is too small. But you can do it while I'm gone to class."

Baby Kate Wheeler. Long bones, long undulations, arms swinging free, gold hair like Hailey's, the sweetest voice in the world, a voice like music. Why couldn't her father love her? He loves me, an ugly older sister whose only grace is that I can read his books. Hailey Wheeler, poet, novelist, Memphis, Tennessee's bright troubled darling son.

I read his books and I loved his wife, Baby Kate and Cauley's mother. I loved her every drunken moment she was here, every drunken afternoon and night until she died.

I found the body myself, or found it seconds after Celestine. I was the one to wipe the vomit off the pillow before the others came.

The coroner was "worried" about that, as he told me several times in the mess that followed. "Not deeply worried," as he said. "Troubled. Of course, we all knew Mrs. Wheeler drank."

Anyway, Hailey loved me and I wasn't beautiful in any part so why couldn't he love his daughter, or pretend to love her, or say he loved her or even quit criticizing her long enough to let her love herself? She spent more time getting dressed than anyone I have ever known.

"If only I were prettier," she was always saying. "If only my face wasn't so thin. If only I had been a beauty like my mother."

Hailey was sitting in the police chaplain's car when I drove up. He was in the backseat with his head bowed. This little shabby-looking chaplain was up front turned around to him on the seat, his hands on the seat belt. I didn't know what to do. I decided to wait. "They took the guy away already." A black girl perched on top of a Peugeot bicycle was holding court on the sidewalk facing the murder door. A white frame house with a porch and a central door framed by windows. You could see men standing in the yellow light through the gauze curtains. The sun was going down behind the roof. The black girl spoke again. "She's lying in the doorway. They have to step over her every time they go in. You watch when they open the door. You can see her feet or something covered with a sheet. She's right there. It could have been an accident."

* * *

"Aunt Allie, you must believe me I am doing all I can to keep it at bay." That's what she told me in the beginning. "I keep talking all the time and I barely let him do it to me. I'm not good at doing it with him. I bet he wishes I was a black girl, a passionate woman. I'm trying not to love him. I know I'm trying not to. Something's holding me back." I turned from the stove where I was making breakfast. It must have been a Sunday, right after she moved in with me. Before they got the place on T. "Then why are you doing it at all?"

"I have to," she said. "I just have to."

So I let them use my apartment all those weeks and the blood is on my hands as surely as it is on his. I could bathe in Clorox and never take the blood away. The blood and the musk and her voice talking to me on the phone and me believing every word she said. Why didn't I go and drag her out of there? Where was my mind? What took my mind away?

There were no beatings here. That started after she went to T Street to be his wife. Oh, yes, she married him. That's how the Wheelers do things. Went down the day before they moved in together and said, I do. She was paying for everything by then, even her own ring. She had that income from the Delta land. Not much, but it must have seemed like a lot to him.

Did I know what was coming? Did Hailey know? Answer: we all know everything. It's just a matter of how much of it we're going to let drift up into our conscious minds at any given moment. At least she didn't die in that mausoleum called Summertree. Where the rest of them finished their drunken lives. Three generations of drunks. That's the real history of this family. I escaped by being ugly. Hailey tried to write his way out. Well, it got us too at last.

Here's the tradition Baby Kate found herself in. Her mother choked to death on absinthe and vomit. She should have stuck to bourbon. She could put bourbon away. Memphis. Nobody loves it, it's a hard town. Are they better off in Boston? I don't know. Same old sun, same old rain, same old longing. All is longing, the Buddha said. I don't believe any of that Eastern stuff, do you?

Baby Kate. When she was small I would dress her up and take her for walks or to the park or to shows the auxiliary put on to raise money. The first telephone number she learned was mine. She would call me when she needed me. Why can't I grieve? How long till I begin to cry? Why did I leave the cemetery before they even lowered the box into the ground? She would have waited for me. She would have stood there until every shovelful was patted down. She was a patient child, a patient girl.

How was it then? Did he come up to her and grab her around the waist with those enormous arms and laugh down into her face and snap her back like a soda cracker? Is that how it was? Did she look up into his face and acquiesce, that way she had of agreeing to things, did she allow her death? The coroner kept walking down the stairs and going up to the uniformed officers and moving his arms up and down, and now the whole thing is lying in the ground that was my baby. How do I go on as if the world is a place of goodness and mercy? How will I prepare?

*   *   *

I'm tired. I'm fifty-four. I'm going to take that post at Belhaven and get an unpublished telephone number. If I go on. Dark, dark, dark. "Come and get me, Allie," she would say in her little voice. "I need you to come get me." Meaning Sally was breaking the dining-room furniture into pieces or melting Hailey's phonograph records in the oven or throwing a television set out of a third-floor window or running naked through the streets, a few of the things she did that I was called in on.

Sally, Sally, Sally, she was so very beautiful. Even at the last, constantly drunk and full of vitriol and screaming insults even at me or anyone she could get to stay on the phone. In repose, the mouth would begin its trembling, that imperceptible tremor, and those violet eyes would pin you down. "Help me, Allie. Why can't you help me?" She choked to death in that bed that had been the general's.

Now it's Baby Kate's turn and Hailey isn't talking to anyone, not even to me, and Franke Brown's in jail that probably wasn't even a bad man and I wouldn't talk about it either except I have to. I can't get rid of it until it's told. She had this little banjo. She would sit on the steps and sing "Rabbit in a Gum Tree, Coon in a Holler." Of course he must have loved her, even if he killed her. She was a princess, a king's child, thrown down upon his bed like a ransom.

I would go to the jail and visit him just to have someone to talk about it to. What did you do to her? I'd say. How did you do it? How could it happen? Say you did not mean to hurt her. No one could want to hurt her. Could they? Could they?

II

Hailey came home from the University of Virginia in the
summer of 1953 and asked Sally Peets to marry him and
she did. They were both drunk at the wedding and Shine
Phillips handcuffed himself to her at the reception and they
had to take him along to the Peabody until someone found
a sheriff with a key. Harvey Trump had wanted to marry
her, as later Harvey Junior wanted to marry Baby Kate.
They own this town, the Trumps do. Baby Kate wouldn't
let him press his body against her, even at a dance. "He's a
fairy," she said. "He smells like a girl."

She could have had any of them at first, until she went
off to Newcomb and got in all that mess. After that it nar-
rowed down and she came home and enrolled at Memphis
State and started drinking at night with English department people who idolized her father. She'd get drunk and
tell them how cold he was to her and they would eat it up.
Knowing Hailey was a bad father made up to them for his
books. The books did all right. He was "legit," as he was
fond of saying. Of course that wasn't what he wanted. He
wanted to be great.

The black girl was perched precariously on the seat of
the Peugeot with her feet on the back wheel. Only the kick-
stand was holding her up. The good-looking coroner in the
beige suit and the built-up heels kept running in and out of
the house conferring with the uniformed policeman, telling
them what the men inside were figuring out. He was so
angry, I loved him for being angry. I could not get mad. I
could not register this death. This death was one too many,
all I wanted to do all afternoon was laugh.

The coroner kept stepping over the obstruction in the
doorway and coming out and going over to the policemen

and raising his arms like wings and snapping them down like he was breaking somebody's back. Let it be her neck, I'd think each time he did it. Not her back. Not her precious back.

The crowd around the Peugeot. Mothers and their children. The sun going down behind the death house. A long time seemed to be going by. Mosquitoes began to bite. An old friend of Baby Kate's named Saint John Wells came walking up the sidewalk wearing a white T-shirt. He was coming to borrow some dope. He didn't have the vaguest notion what he was walking into. There were police cars all over the place. He just kept walking up, smiling like an idiot. What was he smiling about? Hailey got out of the chaplain's car and ran out into the street and grabbed Saint John and started crying in his arms. A mother slapped a child for pointing. "Don't point," she said, in a cold tight voice.

"I'm scared," the child said.

"You have a right to be," I said. I patted the child on the shoulder and went over and took my brother's hand but he was burrowed into Saint John's faded T-shirt. "She's dead," he kept saying. "She's dead. A nigger killed her."

All those weeks they were doing it in my apartment. He was so nice, as nice as he could be. Helpful, bringing flowers and wine. He told me he'd been in some trouble. "What happened?" I asked Baby Kate later. "What was he talking about?"

"He fixes apartments. He buys one and fixes it up, then sells it and buys another one. The reason he got in trouble with the law was someone burned one down and tried to blame it on him. Black people have so much trouble when something like that happens. They can't just call a lawyer

like we do. So he lost a lot of money. He's just starting
over."

"How does he have so much free time in the daytime?"

"He makes it up at night. Don't you notice he isn't
around much at night?"

"Oh," I said. "Of course. I understand."

The faces around the Peugeot. They didn't care. They
didn't give a damn. They weren't surprised. What had
they heard? What had been going on? What did they
know?

"It's going to be on Channel Six at ten," the man from
the panel truck was saying to the rest. "You can see it
then."

Anybody in my family could tell a version of this. This is
the real story. Of whiskey and slaves and bored women and
death. Two hundred years of slavery and still going on and
still paying for it.

Here's the way it was. Here's the first thing I see when I
try to understand, try to find a series of events to follow.
That house, Summertree at the end of the cold lawns.
Sally, drunk in the den, the stereo blaring, Leontyne Price
singing Aida. Hailey writing in his den, standing at a
stand-up desk, reminiscent of you-know-who. Big glass of
bourbon by his side, you-know-who, long half-comprehen-
sible sentences, you-know-who. The servants smoking on
the back veranda. Baby Kate on her little wooden rocking
horse. Black faces all around her. She is eating a Popsicle,
or a bowl of potato chips, anything she wants.

"Come on, honey," I would say and she would drag the
wooden horse across the floor and take it with us.

*   *   *

I am watching my angel die. Through that door. Every time the good-looking clubfooted coroner steps over the door. "It's right there," the girl on the Peugeot says. "It's right in the doorway. They said he beat her with a horse. They took it off when they took him. Some horse toy."

I walk over to the girl. "Don't say any more about this," I say. "Get out of here. All of you, get out of here. That's my niece over there. That dead child is my angel. My baby, my little girl. Get out of here. Get the hell out of here." I am yelling now. At all of them, at every one of them. "Go back inside your houses. Stop watching this. How dare you be here. You goddamn stupid worthless pointless television-watching idiots, get back inside, get out of my sight. I cannot bear the sight of you."

Three officers had me by the arms. The chaplain spoke, "Why are you so angry?" the chaplain said. "Why are you so full of anger?"

"Oh, Allie," Hailey was right behind them. "For God's sake, don't make a scene."

III

The first time Franke beat her up was not in my apartment. It was in July after the cocktail party she dragged him to at the museum.

"It was my fault," she told me. We were in my car. I was taking her to the dentist to get her teeth fixed. "I took him there to show him off. To make them look at him. It wasn't fair. It wasn't his fault. I forgive him."

"No," I said. "Forgiveness is for what you can't understand. You are part of this. If you understand, you are part of it. Are you part of it, Baby Kate? Of beating yourself up? Of breaking your teeth? Didn't you have enough of that when your mother was alive?"

"I don't care. It doesn't matter. Those are only words. I love him, which is not words, which is real. Which I will stand by."

"You must go to her," I told Hailey. "He beat her up. He broke two of her teeth."

"She has made her bed," he said. "I'm done with it. Done with her."

"No, you have to intervene. Someone has to."

"Leave me alone," he said. He went upstairs. I heard the door to his office close like a coffin lid. I went out onto the back porch looking for her old horse. "Where's that wooden horse of Miss Baby Kate's?" I said to Celestine, who was sitting at the table pretending to shell peas. "Where'd you put her horse?"

"It's upstairs on the third floor with her stuff. He said not to let her have none of it."

"Well, I'm getting that horse." I went upstairs and found it on top of some boxes of books and picked it up. It was a wonderful hand-carved creature, a golden palomino with a dark gold mane and a red saddle with a design like coins. Where the paint had chipped away above the eyes the dark grain of the wood showed through. Mahogany or cypress. I patted it on the head. It will bring her to her senses, I decided. It will remind her to ride away.

I picked it up and carried it down the stairs, my mother's stairs, my grandmother's stairs. What is that law? Primogeniture? I'm getting so bad about language. I can't remember the words I need. I carried the horse down the stairs and out to my car. When she was little she would set it up in my front hall and pretend to be out West. "Dat West," she called it. "I'm at dat West, Allie, bring me dat sandwich den." And I would pretend to be the old chuckwagon cook and serve her wild steer and Nebraska grass and buffalo and she would ride "dem hills." "I'm widing dem hills some more," she would call out and I would say, "Slow down, slow down."

"He has confessed," Channel Six informs me. "Wife murderer begs to be allowed to go to funeral. Family refuses his request." Confess, what does that mean? What did he say? What did he say he did to her? Have the gravediggers covered the grave?

I dreamed last night the coffin was sitting beside the grave and all the people left the cemetery and when they were gone the funeral parlor came and took the coffin back to their store and opened it and took her out and returned her to us.

"What a tacky dress," she said. "It's torn all the way up the back. Someone get me something else to wear."

"I will make you a dress of cowslips," I said. "A dress of blue flowers."

The second time he beat her up was on the Mississippi coast, at Hailey's spare house in Biloxi. They had gone down there without permission. The caretaker was rude to them. He called Hailey. He told them they could only stay one night. Then they were treated badly in a seafood restaurant. The waitress wouldn't bring them a menu. Baby Kate was scared. She acted badly. Afterwards he took her to a black oyster bar. She danced with the owner. They walked out on the dunes. Franke hit her in the face. He threw her down in the sand and left her there and took her car and drove home alone.

She came to me. She stayed two days. She got up at twelve o'clock the third night and went back to him. She

called a cab and went back to T Street. "I made him do it,"
she said. "I pretended I didn't know him. I flirted with his
friend."

"You can't go back over there. I won't let you go." I had
thrown myself in front of the door. "You are not going back
over there." She pushed me out of her way. "I am his wife. I
am going to sleep where he is every night of my life. As long
as I live I will wake up at his side. I am married to him. I
am his woman. Let me go, Allie." And she pushed past me
wearing a raincoat over her nightgown and went out into
the night and I did not see her after that until I saw her
dead. Although she called me. "I'm fine," she said when she
called. "We're both working. We're doing fine."

"I'm coming over there and see about you. Tell me the
address."

"Don't come here. Don't any of you come here. I don't
want you here." She paused. "It would get me in trouble."

"What do you mean, in trouble? In what kind of trouble?
What's going on, Baby Kate? Tell me what's going on."

"I have to go now, Allie. I have to start dinner. He'll be
home in a while." She was going away. And I could not
hold her.

"What are you doing? Tell me what you do."

"At night we lie on the floor and listen to the crickets and
the sound of the people in the neighborhood and I tell him
my stories and he tells me his. We will never run out of
stories. We are married, Allie. He is my husband."

"I have your rocking horse. I got it from your father's.
Don't you want it? For a planter. Or in case some children
come to visit. You could put it on a porch. Do you have a
porch?"

"I don't need it now."

"Don't you want anything from us? Don't you want to even know we're here?"

"Meet me at the corner of Line and Randolph tomorrow at noon. I'll come and get it from you there."

"What's going on, Baby Kate? What are you doing? Why can't I come to your house?"

"Will you meet me there? It's a Wal-Mart. I'll be by the main door."

"Of course I will. At twelve then." I was there at eleven-thirty. Pacing up and down the sidewalk in my Red Cross shoes. At ten to twelve he came and took the horse from me. "She had to work," he said. "She said to tell you she tried to call. You'd already left."

"Is she all right, Franke? Are you all right? Do you have everything you need?"

"We're doing good. We're doing fine. I'm teaching her to cook. We're doing fine. Yes, we are." He drove off in her car. He was wearing a white visor, a white shirt with long sleeves. I don't believe the world I lived to see.

Perhaps I will go and visit him in the jail. What could he tell me? He could say he didn't mean to do it. He could say it was an accident. If it was an accident I might be able to watch the evening news again, to care about my fellow man. Black people. We brought them here. Someone did. Not me. We are being punished forever, the bringers and the brought. Tautologies, old clichés, pray for us all. Pray for the world.

The crowd has thinned. The girl on the Peugeot rides off down the street. The man climbs back into his van. The whining girl goes in to bed. The chaplain gets out of his car carrying a child's carseat and stows it in the trunk. Saint John wipes his hands on his T-shirt.

I'm starting to laugh. I've been wanting to laugh for hours.

The white house seems to float above the street. "Is this a bad neighborhood?" a woman says. "I have to know. I just moved here."

"I don't know," I tell her. "I'm sorry. I just don't know."

The Young Man

THIS IS A story about an old lady who ordered a young man from an L. L. Bean catalog. He was a nice young man with wide shoulders and a worried smile. He had on a tweed coat and dark tan pants and a nice-looking tie with little squiggly things all over it. His fingernails were clean and his hair neatly combed. He liked to work but he was also a good companion on trips. His table manners were excellent but not noticeable. He liked to talk but knew how to let the other person have their turn. Mrs. Bradlee never did get around to asking him what his profession was, his line of work. There never did seem to be a polite way to ask.

All of Mrs. Bradlee's friends were getting young men. You could hardly find four for bridge anymore at the Recess Club. Fanny Hawkins had even started dressing like her young man, flat shoes and work pants. Carrie Hatcher pretended her young man was a chauffeur. All they did was drive around talking about themselves. Elsie Whitfield stayed on the coast with hers; they went fishing. It made Mrs. Bradlee sick at her stomach to think of it. One night she dreamed a big Greyhound bus pulled up in front of the old courthouse on State Street and all these young men got out and started spreading out all over Jackson, moving out in all directions. Like a web that had fallen over the world.

Mrs. Bradlee wasn't having anything to do with it. They weren't eating dinner at her house. I've seen enough, she told herself. I've had enough to contend with. Mrs. Bradlee was a widow. She had buried two sons in two wars and a husband from smoking cigarettes. All I want to do from now on is live a normal life, she told her remaining children. So whatever you do, don't tell me about it. Just come over on Sunday after church while you're still covered up.

You shouldn't live alone, her friends were always telling Mrs. Bradlee. She still lived in her house on Lakefront Drive, with all her rooms. They wanted her to get an apartment where they were, at Westchester Arms, or Dunleith Court or Dunsinae Towers. Well, she wasn't going to move into an apartment. She wasn't joining the herd. She had been raised in the country. She had seen one cow lead the rest to water. Still, it was getting lonely in the big stone house. If only it could be like it used to be, with her friends coming over for cards. They had even started bringing the young men to Saint James. Right up to the prayer rail, and beyond. Alece Treadway was sending hers to divinity school.

It was too much. In the past Mrs. Bradlee had been known as the leader. She had been the first to cut her hair

at college, the first to have a white cook, the first to get a
face-lift (when the time came), the first to visit behind the
Iron Curtain. When August, her husband, was still alive.
Now, with their craze for young men, the crowd had left
her behind.

It was all so, well, so messy. And the young men themselves, well, she hated to cast stones, but they were messy
too. Well, they were. They wore open-collar sport shirts and
tennis sneakers and barely cut their hair. It was too much.
It was just too much. Mrs. Bradlee's knitting needles
clicked like a thousand crickets. She was alone in her living
room. A beautiful sunset was covering the lake with her favorite shades of blue and pink. Elvie Howard had bowed
out of their Wednesday night canasta game, now that she
had her swimming pool maintenance friend. He has a degree in Philosophy, she told Mrs. Bradlee, from the East.
It's television, Mrs. Bradlee decided. That's where they got
the ideas. She switched off her own and went into the library to read.

A stack of catalogs was on a table by the windowseat. She
began flipping through them, thinking of ordering some
clothes for the grandchildren for Christmas. She took a
piece of white chocolate from a dish and began to nibble on
it, looking at the elegant clothes and shoes and hand-carved
decoys, the scarves and ties and stacks of well-made shirts.
One model began to catch her eye. He was in several different catalogs. The best picture was on page sixteen of the L.
L. Bean catalog. He had such neat hair, his smile was so,
well, just right, not too smiley, just enough so you would
know he was friendly. His hands were in his pockets. He
was standing so tall and straight. I ought to order him, she

thought. Laughing to herself out loud. She ate another piece of chocolate. Then another. Hello, she said to the photograph. What's your name?

It was growing dark outside. She pushed a light switch and carried the catalog over to a desk and sat down and took an order blank out of the back and began to fill it in. *One,* she wrote, page 16, number 331, color, white, she paused at where to fill in the amount. $10,000, she wrote and added her Merrill Lynch Visa Card number. There, that should be about right. She folded the order blank in halves, stuck it into its envelope, and carried it across the room to the marble table before the fireplace. She dropped it on a silver salver. Here, Mr. Postman, she said, as if she were a child playing at things, take this letter to the warehouse.

A bell was ringing in the hall. The cook was calling her to dinner.

In the morning the envelope was gone. "Have you seen an envelope I left in the library?" she said to the maid. "Well, yes, I did," the girl said. "I mailed it for you. In the morning mail."

"Oh, you can't mail that," Mrs. Bradlee said. "It was a joke. Those people will think I'm crazy when they open that. They'll say, here's a woman in Mississippi who's lost her mind."

"What was it, ma'am?" the maid said.

"I ordered something they don't sell," she said. The two of them laughed together at that. Mrs. Bradlee liked the little maid. An octoroon named Rivers, a sweet girl who was always neat and clean and smelled good.

*   *   *

It was a week later when the young man came. It was nine in the morning. A Sunday morning. Mrs. Bradlee had been up and dressed for an hour, enjoying the fall colors out the windows. She saw him coming up the walk. "You ordered me," he said. "And here I am."

"Go away," she said.

"I can't," he said. "I belong here now. You asked for me. I don't have anyplace else to be."

"Have you had breakfast?" she said.

"No," he said.

"Come in," she said. "I will feed you." It was warm in the breakfast room, filled with morning sunlight. "Do you mind if I take off my coat?" he said. "Oh, no," she answered. "Here, let me take it for you." She took the lovely tweed coat and laid it across an empty chair. It was the cook's day off. She fixed eggs and toast and juice. When he was finished he laid his fork and knife neatly along the edge of the plate. "If you'll excuse me now," he said. "I would like to use your bathroom.'

She led the way to the guest room. When he returned she suggested that they go to church. "Mr. Biggs, our choir director, has a special musicale this morning. After morning prayer. You might enjoy that."

"It will be fine," he said. "I'm sure I'll think it's just right."

You should have seen the eyes when Mrs. Bradlee walked in with him, walked right up front to her regular pew and he helped her in and pulled down the prayer bench and knelt beside her. Thank you, she heard herself pray, you know I deserved this. The music was grand, clear and cold water running over stones. The whole church and all its people melded together by music, one big melodic pyramid. Afterwards, they stood outside and Mrs. Bradlee introduced him all around.

In the afternoon they took naps in their rooms, then went for a walk around the grounds, down to the lake, and back to the house. He walked at just the right rate of speed, not running ahead of her all the time like August did, saying can't you keep up, if you didn't talk so much you could keep up with me. Larry didn't mind how much Mrs. Bradlee talked. He was interested in everything she said.

"How long are you staying?" she asked finally. It was after dinner. They were having coffee in the den. It seemed like the proper thing to say.

"How long did you want me for?" he asked. He was looking straight at her out of his dark blue eyes. He was looking at her as if there were no wrong answers.

"Let me think about it," she said. "I'm still getting used to the idea."

"Fine," he said. "Whatever you say."

"Where would you go if you left here? Where else would you be?"

"I wouldn't be," he said. "There is only here."

"And you don't mind," she said.

"Why should I mind?" he answered. "That's the way it is."

"I'm going to bed now," she said. "I need to sleep."

"Goodnight then," he said. "I'll see you in the morning."

In the morning it was Monday. She dressed before she went downstairs. They had breakfast. "Now you should go to work," she said. "It's Monday morning."

"Fine," he said. "I'll be back at five-thirty."

"Take the blue car," she said. "I don't use it."

"I will," he said. "I like cars to be blue. It's my favorite color." After he was gone Mrs. Bradlee talked on the phone all morning. All her friends called her one by one. What's he like, they asked. He likes blue, she answered. His favorite color is blue. Go fishing with us, Elsie Whitfield said. We might, Mrs. Bradlee answered. I'll have to see. Do you want to? she asked him later. I don't know, he said. Do you? I don't think so, she said. It's so messy. Find a nice way to tell them, he said. Don't hurt their feelings.

Don't you need some other clothes, she said. You might grow tired of that coat. That will be nice, he said. We'll go shopping at the mall.

Many days went by. Many weeks. Christmas came and went. They gave each other gifts. He gave her a bracelet with her name inside. She gave him a bundle of fatwood sticks she ordered from Maine and a tiny sled containing a gold watch. He put it on. His wrist was so perfect. The hair lay so softly along the flesh. Mrs. Bradlee drew in her breath. For a moment she wanted to kiss his hand. God is love, she thought, and reached out to touch his hand instead. We might go to Switzerland for a month, she said. That would be nice, he said. I think that would be perfect.

In January the rain fell and the Pearl River rose and the cold came and stayed. It got into Mrs. Bradlee's bones. She felt tired even in the mornings. Her appetite was not good. When she passed Larry in the hall she sighed. He was there every morning. He was there every afternoon. Every Friday she filled the blue car up with gasoline. Every month the bills came. Every morning after breakfast he disappeared into the guest room. It made her sick at her stomach to think what he did in there.

She began to be cold to him. She was quiet when they went on walks. She stopped telling him everything. After all, what had he ever told her? She was giving him all her stories. In return, all he knew was blue. Blue skies, blue, blue, blue.

"I think you should play the piano," she told him one evening. "It would be a good idea for you to play."

"I'm not a piano player," he said. "That isn't what you asked for."

"You could learn, couldn't you? You could take lessons."

"I'll try," he said. "I'll be glad to try."

"It should sound like this," she said. She took a Mozart sonata out of its cover and put it on the record player. It was sonata number 13 in B major, played by Wanda Landowska. "But that's a woman playing," he said.

"It doesn't matter," Mrs. Bradlee said. "It's all the same thing."

He wasn't any good at the piano. He took lessons for three months but nothing happened. His hands were better in his pockets. His hands were better taking the Maine fatwood and using it to light the library fires at night. They were nice laying his knife and fork across his plate after meals. They were too large for the piano or too stiff or too short. Something was wrong. You're disappointed, aren't you, he said at last. Yes, she answered, to tell the truth I am. I think you will have to leave soon. It isn't a good idea anymore. You will have to find somewhere else to go.

How long should I stay, he asked. I don't know the right amount of time.

Until Easter weekend, she said. That should be about right.

Maundy Thursday came. They met for breakfast without speaking of it. He looked pale. Eat, she said. You should eat before your journey.

On Good Friday they went to communion. He looks tired, Fanny Hawkins said to her. He looks like he needs a rest.

On Holy Saturday he walked all around the house, all day, out into the yard, and down along the river. He looked very beautiful, and light. He had not gone into the guest room after breakfast. He had barely eaten anything at all. Mrs. Bradlee was beginning to enjoy him again. He seemed so light, so easy to support.

Perhaps I'll have him stay till summer, she thought, watching his progress across the yard; he was moving toward a line of dogwood trees set against the horizon. Three trees against a blue sky. Yes, I will tell him we will think it over.

The phone rang. It was the refrigerator repairman. What a time to call, she told him. Come Monday. Don't worry about it now. It broke her concentration. She went back to her afghan. She was knitting an afghan to sell at a church bazaar. When Larry came in he walked by without speaking. He did not come down to dinner. I'll talk to him later, she thought. The meal was heavy. She drank too much wine and fell asleep earlier than she expected.

In the morning she went to find him. Of course he was not there. She looked all over the house. She looked in all the closets. She looked in the basement and the wine cellar and the attic. She went out into the garage and looked in the blue car. She went to the guest room. She stood in the door. There was nothing there. The door to the guest-room powder room was open. I could look in there, she thought. But I'm not going to.

She went out into the hall and sat down on the stairs. She

listened for the sound of footsteps. She thought about the stars. She said the alphabet over and over to herself. It was a trick she had practiced as a child to pass the time. After a while she went down to the library and got out the new catalogs and began to look through them. I might get a young woman this time, she thought. It was a gay thought. How brave, they would all say. A young woman with all the things that can go wrong. I would like a tall one with a long waist, she decided. Long legs and a long waist. A singing voice. Piano skills.

First Manhattans

THE SEDUCTION of Annalisa Livingston by her black chauffeur, Kenneth Williams, of Laurel, Mississippi and New York City, New York. And/or, the seduction of Kenny Williams by his employer and older mentor, Annalisa Livingston of Mobile, Alabama and New York City, New York. Some events that happened during a week when the moon was so near the earth it was even affecting people in New York City. Events that happened in the spring of nineteen hundred and eighty-four, long after the social experiments of the sixties had cooled down and people in the United States had gone back to fucking people who resembled their own parents.

Let us begin on a Sunday morning in early spring, in an apartment on East Seventy-third between Second and Third Avenues. A wind has blown all night from the ocean,

cleaning off the city, the sun is just beginning to light up
the East River, traffic has begun to move, Annalisa is asleep
in her white enamel four-poster bed. She is dreaming a re-
current dream. A huge choir robed in white fills the streets
of New York City. They are singing her favorite hymn. "I
sing a song of the saints of the Lord, . . . and one was a doctor and one was a priest and one was eaten by a fierce wild
beast . . ." da, da, da . . . a lion appears among the people.
He turns and sniffs the air, then looks at Annalisa. He starts
her way. His jaws open wide.

She woke up in a sweat, threw the covers on the floor.
Adrenaline? Insulin shock? No, too much cover, too many
chocolates at midnight. Desist, she counseled herself. Don't
be a fool. She sat up, looked around the room. The sun was
up. A soft diffused light was coming in around the edges of
the curtains. Soft, grayish yellow light all over the bedside
tables piled high with bric-a-brac and church programs.
Lamps in the shape of china shepherdesses stood up among
the small, neatly folded, accordion-pleated, twisted, scrib-
bled on, white and pastel souvenirs of Annalisa's work.

What time is it? she wondered. She pulled a watch out
from under some typed pages. Six-fifteen. She sat up,
counted on her fingers. Saint Alban's at seven. Saint Mark's
at nine. Saint James the Lesser at eleven. No, the cathedral.
Bishop Green from New Haven. Then Evensong. Oh, that
was too much. Evensong at three. Who ever heard of such a
thing. Cutting church schedules to the cloth of modern life.
Well, it was all wrong and Annalisa was going to tell them
so.

That was her job. She was the church critic for the *New
York Times*. She was the one who told them where to go and

who to listen to. She was the hottest thing in town, the one everyone was reading. This month she was taking on the Episcopalians, now in the grips of a mighty influx of status seekers and social climbers. Annalisa had been laying low on the Episcopalians. Now, their turn had come.

She grabbed a legal pad from under a pair of underpants and being scribbling. "Evensong in the middle of the afternoon. What the new prayer book left undone this sort of trifling will polish off like a sort of spiritual chocolate mousse." She dropped the legal pad on the bed, went into the bathroom, threw water on her face, ran a comb through her hair, came back into the bedroom and started getting dressed. Where's my navy dress, she asked herself. It's around here somewhere. I'll cut out Saint James. Still, if I don't go Marvin Fannin might be there, and they are having that anarchist. Well, damn. She finished dressing, found her pocketbook and was out the door. Stop thinking about Marvin Fannin, she told herself. You invented the genre, you set the standards, you defined the terms. She was in the elevator, adjusting her blouse, putting on her earrings. No one can catch up with you. You are Annalisa Livingston, the one who compared Doctor Whitlaw to Cotton Mather, who got Eighth Avenue Presbyterian to refinish its pews, who called upon the Church of the Latter-Day Saints to get those boys some new suits.

The elevator was going down. She caressed her legs, her thighs, surprised they were still there. She had not had a lover in months. She had been consumed with glory and left her libido to shrivel up, alone in a corner sweeping ashes. My poor libido, she thought as she touched her hips. What a way to live. Well, never mind. I haven't got time for that. Oh, what did Josh Lyons say about me in his column?

A religious Dorothy Parker with the dedication of Bishop Sheen.

"Miss Livingston! Annalisa, over here! Look over here." It was Kenny. He unfolded his six feet four inches of dark chocolate gorgeousness out of his cab and came around and opened the door. He was wearing white slacks, a baby blue polo shirt, white shoes and his Raybans. "I was getting worried," he said. "I thought something must have happened to you."

"Oh, Kenny," she said. "I don't know what I'd do without you." He put her into the cab and slid himself into the driver's seat.

"I was about to come up there and see what was going on. Next time, lean out the window and holler at me if you're going to be late."

"I will. I'm sorry. I overslept."

"Well, let's get going then. Don't worry, I'll get you there."

He spun the taxi around the corner of Sixty-fourth and Second Avenue, found a lane and leaped forward with a burst of speed. Kenny drove as he lived. He had the heart of a sprinter. He would lay low, then break into action. There was that in Annalisa too. She barely noticed as they cruised and lurched their way around the city. "That was a great piece you did on the Presbyterians," he said. "I laughed my head off at that one part. I cut it out to send my brother in Chicago. Now I wish I had it back. You got an extra copy?"

Annalisa held on to the change cup, leaning up into the front seat. "What part? What part did you think was funny?"

"About the Presbyterians got old eyes. That was the part."

"Oh, about presmyopia of the soul. That was pretty good, wasn't it? They'll kill me in Mobile for writing that."

"That guy at the *Post*. He can't touch it. You not worrying about him anymore, are you?"

"There are always imitators, Kenny. People have always copied me. It's not the first time I've run into this. Look, turn down Fifty-first if you can. Come up under the porte cochere. No, don't worry about Marvin Fannin."

"You showed him to me once. Remember, at that thing in the park. That preach-off, or whatever you call it. You showed him to me and his buddy he was with. You said to see if I thought he was a man."

"Oh, yes. I'd forgotten that. Look, Kenny, there's the church. Slow down. I don't want to come tearing down the street. There, by that awning. Who's that out front? Is that the priest?" She fished around in her purse for her glasses, found them and settled them on her nose. Everything came into focus, lines on the sidewalk, leaves on the trees. The priest was a round-faced young woman in a dark dress with a white collar. About thirty pounds overweight. The role of oral pleasures in the life of the clergy, Annalisa thought. The sin of gluttony. Break fast. The communion wafer against the palate, the sweet wine breaking the long night's fast. Very clever, how they wouldn't let you eat until they fed you. This is my body which is broken for you, take, eat. This is my blood of the new testament which is shed for you and for many for the remission of sins. Drink ye all of it. They should try using doughnuts or sweet rolls. Yes, think of it. The priest would be passing a plate of tiny white powdered doughnuts. Choice of white or chocolate milk. We'd see if the mystery would hold up against that competition. Here is my doughnut which is broken for you. . . .

"So glad to have you here," the young woman said, helping her from the cab. "It's so nice of you to come. I won't be doing a sermon, of course. Just a very small bid for peace between the Creed and the Sentences. I'm really pretty much of a traditionalist. I've noticed you like that, don't you?" She smiled into Annalisa's eyes. Her soft white hand floated in Annalisa's hand. Blood of the lamb. Blood of the lamb. Oh, it was all too easy to be fun anymore. "I'd go back to the old prayer book if it was up to me," the woman continued. "All the way, but what can you do?"

"Let me sit near the back," Annalisa said. "So I can view the whole thing. Your voice carries?"

"Oh, yes, I never use a mike."

Kenny was waiting at the curb when she came out. Leaning against the cab, his Raybans pushed up on his head. Annalisa was surrounded by people. "Well, that's really awfully kind of you," she was saying, trying to get away. "I'm sure I'd love to read it. Send it to me at the paper. Oh, of course. I'm so glad you approved," she smiled at Kenny. He smiled back and whisked her into the cab.

"Jesus Christ," she began. "You won't believe what that woman has going on in there. A lute player instead of an organ. Not even an altar boy. The oldest Episcopal church in Manhattan. Can you believe it?"

"Didn't look like much of a crowd to me. Maybe they can't afford nothing else."

"Altar boys are free. Well, take me home. I need to change shoes before the nine o'clock."

"What's wrong with the ones you got on. They look nice."

"The heels are too low. You don't think I have time to change?"

"I think you ought to get you a bite to eat instead. You seem mighty high-strung to me this morning. I'd eat a bite if I was you."

"All right. Run by a deli then. Get some coffee and a roll. Some mornings I wish I'd never started this, Kenny. Some days I think I've lost my mind."

"Oh, don't say that, Annalisa." He turned around in his seat. "You the church critic. You got folks out there counting on you. You can't give up now."

"I know," she said. She sighed and leaned back against the seat, considering her destiny. Kenny returned his eyes to the road. His hands gripped the wheel, his wide shoulders swayed with the car. He considered it too, Annalisa's mission, and his role as her protector. They cruised in peace for a few blocks. Annalisa imagined the car she would get for him to drive someday. A Citroën. Or a Peugeot. He would always wear his regular clothes, never a uniform. Her best friend is her black driver, they would say. Yes, a very black man, not a mulatto. Yes, she lives her Christianity. It's what makes her what she is. Not the jewel-like paragraphs and dazzling insights. No, it's the pure heart that drives the pen.

Annalisa leaned back in the seat, thinking of pieces from her columns.

Concerning the single most presumptuous trespass I have ever had the misfortune to witness or hear. First Baptist has rewritten the words to "The Church's One Foundation." A Mrs. Sue Gay Trillium is credited with the new lyrics, which include such images as "the eyes of life are upon you," and "clean blood of new Christ battens death."

I left during the second verse but the strains of the organ pursued me into the parking lot and have haunted me for days.

In a time when visions of God are usually connected with world hunger or justice for the poor, Saint Simon's has decorated its vestments with fourteen-carat gold lamé. In a neighborhood of soup kitchens this can only be called childishly bad taste.

No. No. No. A sermon in the middle of a wedding. Three ordained ministers on the altar accompanied by a bearded man an usher informed me was the bride's analyst.

The wedding sermon called upon us to view marriage as the salt of the earth. Not salt, the minister assured us, as in the substance, *we now know to be harmful* and *fattening* to our bodies, but salt, as in leavening, by which we are kept afloat.

Someone must be held responsible when such statements are made in the presence of children.

Attended a debate last night at the Christian Life Commission over whether hungry people deserve help. The conclusion, after several hours of vigorous discussion, was that hunger is caused by poverty and poverty is caused by people being poor. The commission will reconvene in February.

Saint Philip's of the Lake weekly newspaper, *The Single Times,* ran a lead article this week written by an ex-army chaplain. He said he was in the Korean War and saw the kind of wishy-washy Christianity now being taught *melt in the heat of battle.* "I saw Christian soldiers run," Reverend Monroe said.

Balm in Gilead. I sat behind a six-year-old boy at Grace Methodist last Sunday. He was drawing on a pad during the sermon. He drew a remarkably accurate picture of the

minister and the altar and the ferns. Then he added a bal-
loon coming out of the minister's mouth which said,
"You're fat."

"You want some cream in your coffee?" Kenny said. He
had pulled to a stop before a deli.

"Oh, yes," she said. "Oh, Kenny, all of a sudden it seems
like such a nice day. The air's so clear you can almost
breathe it."

"What you want to eat?"

"A walnut and raisin scone with butter and marmalade.
You are such a dear, so kind to me."

"This day is picking up. When I saw you get off the elevator I thought, oh, oh, this day will be a bitch. Now, look-
a-here, the sun is shining."

"Go on in," she said, retreating. "Go get the coffee." He
left. Annalisa settled back into the seat to go over a list of
sermons for the week. "On the Church's Role in Israel."
Oh, God, she thought. I forgot to call Rabbi Feibelman
back. Well, I'm definitely not getting into that. I am not
doing synagogues. They've got plenty of writers of their
own. They can just get Philip Roth or Saul Bellow or someone. This pace is killing me as it is. Eating breakfast in a
cab. I don't know how I let this happen.

How it happened was one of those wild balloonings that
only happen in a great city hungry for diversions, among a
people with so little real work that words become the whole
experience.

One evening Annalisa left her office at *Woman's World,*
where she worked as uplift editor, and walked over to
Times Square to see a movie. It was dark when she left the
theater, a clear night with many stars. She walked for several blocks, then stopped to rest against the railing of a
Greek Orthodox church. The door was open. She could see

all the way to the altar. The altar cloth was a disgrace,
drooping to one side, dingy and unironed. Disgraceful, she
thought. I should write them a letter. A little epistle. They
should polish up those pews, paint the walls, clean the windows, act like they're proud to be Christians. I'll bet a lot of
churches are going down now that everyone watches it on
TV. *I could write a column.* Go around to different churches
and praise the good ones and admonish the bad and give
advice and check up later to see how they're coming along.
Oh, that would be a good and useful thing to do. It would
be good work, a way to help my fellow man.

She had taken the idea to the religion editor of the *New
York Times.* He was in a slump. There was talk of doing
away with the whole section of the paper and making it an
adjunct of Entertainment. He had a vision of Annalisa as
his savior.

"By God, I'll do it," he said. "We'll call you the Times
Church Mouse."

"Of course not," she said, gathering up her papers as if to
leave. "I am a serious woman, with the gift of faith."

"All About the Churches?"

"Our Lady in Your Pew had occurred to me."

"Done. You can start this week."

"I can't promise you anything, you know. We'll just see
what happens." She sat back in the chair and lowered her
eyes to her hands.

What happened surprised them all. In two weeks "Our
Lady in Your Pew" was the talk of New York City.

"I went to Saint Philip's to a christening this morning," a
woman would say.

"Oh, did you see what Annalisa Livingston said about

the communion cup in Episcopal churches? She said she wouldn't touch it during flu season and advised everybody else to stop too. She said Christian sharing did not include saliva."

"Oh, she's wonderful, isn't she? She's articulating so much stuff. She's saying everything no one will dare to say."

"Lucky for us Martin Luther was not bothered by such scruples," she wrote. And, "the swinging of censers in uptown churches has reached fever pitch. Last week Dean Stamps threw up such a cloud in the cathedral that an elderly woman had to be taken out on a stretcher."

"Myth-augmenters," she called one group. "Ritualdousers," and "the sort of fellowship one finds in taverns," and "pews that need sanding, silver that needs polishing, rhetoric that needs editing."

"She's right on top of it," Buckley said of her in an interview. "Sic 'em, Annalisa. These guys have been getting away with murder for centuries."

"I've been invited to meet Mr. Fannin," she said, when Kenny returned to the cab with the coffee. "To his place in the country to spend the day on Saturday. I'm thinking of going. He used to be a Jesuit, did I tell you that? I might find out some things for my book." She took the little Styrofoam cup Kenny handed her.

"I don't know about getting all buddy-buddy with the competition. I wouldn't do that if I was you."

"Well, I don't know. His secretary called me. It's lonely work, covering churches, Kenny. I mean, who do I have to talk to?"

"You got me."

"I know and it's a blessing. Well, I might go on and meet

Mr. Fannin. I mean, what harm can it do? I'm thinking of writing a book about the Catholic orders and I could use the information. He used to be in one, you know? Jesuits. Anyway, I'm going to call it 'Why Did Their Mothers Let Them Go?' "

"Why their mothers let them go?"

"You know, like why would a woman send her child off to live with a bunch of priests and all. I'm taking the position that it is because many women secretly hate their children. I mean, in nature animals often kill their young. Anyway, I wouldn't tell Mr. Fannin that, of course. Just ask him if he'd like to share some of his memories. Since he left."

"I don't think them Roman Catholics ever get over that stuff. I had this girlfriend once, that was a Roman Catholic. She would pray on them little beads and she wouldn't take the pill. . . ."

"Well, that's enough of that. Anyway, I'm thinking of saying yes. Just so I can ask him about the orders."

"We got to get a move on if we're going to make that nine o'clock." Kenny swung the taxi back out into the traffic. Sunlight poured in the window on Annalisa's hand. She polished off the scone. Wouldn't take the pill? She imagined Kenny in a room with a girl trying to get her to take a pill. The girl was seated on a bed, a small pretty black girl. In her hand was a round plastic birth control pill container. Kenny was leaning over her. "Where is she now?" Annalisa said. "The girl, I mean?"

"Oh, she went back to Atlanta. She didn't like it here."

There was a huge manila envelope by the door when Annalisa got home. It was her fan mail from the paper. There were letters raving about her work. And vicious criticisms. Nothing she had ever done at *Woman's World* had elicited a response from the public. She had to read the letters. She could not keep from doing it. "Is this bitch a hoax?" one said. "Who does she think she is to even write the name of such a fine man as Dean Weller? She would be lucky to have him run over her with his car."

"She is visited like a pox upon the spiritual life of the city," said a third. "The *Times* has lost its mind to print such trash."

"Not since Anatole Broyard and Benjamin Demott took over the *New York Times* Book Review section has such a distortion of values managed to invade the world's best newspaper. Cancel my subscription."

"I am not canceling my subscription but I am definitely registering a complaint. I can't believe the attack on the Commission for Christian Giving and Father Delacroix, who is a saint."

And so on. The mail was running about three to one in her favor but the complaints were on good stationery with impressive letterheads. The mash notes were from ladies with spidery handwriting and flowers on the envelopes. Annalisa wadded up the complaints, then got them back out of the trash can and read them again. The phone rang. It was Marvin Fannin.

"Oh, I'm so glad it's you. I'm in a dreadful mood. I just got my fan mail. A lot of people are very upset that we're attacking the church."

"To hell with them," Marvin said. "Angel, if we listened

to our critics we would never write a word. Burn them up. I mean, darling, who would write a letter to a newspaper? Some boring little people you'd never notice on the street. Now, look, I'm simply dying to meet you and have you come out on Saturday. Only a small crowd and I promise you a divine lunch. Say you'll come. I'll send a car for you."

"Oh, no, I have a car. And, yes, I will come. I want to meet you too. I've liked some of your pieces so much, that article on the Cloisters was perfect."

"Fab-u-lous. At noon then. You've got the address. I'll have a little mappy sent around in the morning. Oh, this is nice. Wait till I tell David."

"David?"

"He's my roommate."

"I'll be there then. At noon?"

"We'll be waiting for you."

Saturday was a beautiful day. Annalisa played music on the radio as she dressed. "Someday he'll come along, the man I love, and he'll be big and strong, the man I love. . . ." She hummed along as she put on white linen slacks, a white silk blouse, a yellow scarf from the Van Gogh exhibition. "Yellow, Pale Saffron, Yellow, Pale Gold, Lemon, How beautiful yellow is. . . ." She tied and retied the scarf around her neck. She had decided to go to the exhibition on the spur of the moment one busy day. She and Kenny had gone together, standing in line for tickets, eating lunch afterwards in the museum cafeteria. Sliced tomatoes and onion soup and cornbread. "Those paintings look like someone that really knew what they was doing drew them," Kenny kept saying. "You can tell the ones that got the in-side track a mile away." He had buttered her cornbread and put it on her plate. "Like in your line of work you're

the best there is. That's why I spend so much time on you."
She thought of him, carefully buttering her cornbread,
using so much butter it dripped off the sides onto the plate.

The drive to the country was quiet. Annalisa fell asleep
and didn't wake until Kenny was turning into a lane leading to a two-story house flanked by elm trees. Marvin was
waiting on the porch, wearing a baby blue sweater. "Well, I
can't believe we meet at last," he said, helping her from the
cab. "It is fab-u-lous of you to come and visit."

Kenny got out and stood at attention. "This is my driver,
Mr. Williams," Annalisa said. "He's going to wait for me."

"Good, good. Go in the kitchen and let them give you
something to drink, Mr. Williams."

"I'll just wait."

"Oh, you can't sit out here all afternoon. Go on inside
and find someone to talk to in the kitchen. The staff will be
glad to see you."

"Kenny!" Annalisa said.

"I got a book to read. I'll just stay here. You go on to
your party, Annalisa. I'll be here if you need me." The dogs
chose that moment to come out the front door and surround them, three large albino Doberman pinschers.
Kenny eased himself back into the cab. "They got some of
them down in Montgomery where my auntie lives," he
said. "People, not dogs. It makes them blind to be so white.
You have trouble with them seeing, Mr. Fannin?"

"No, it doesn't seem to affect their eyesight. Well, come
along, Miss Livingston. Let's go and join the others."
Kenny rolled up the windows and opened his book. *Beyond
the Chains of Illusion,* it was a book Annalisa had given him
for Christmas. "Life itself then is seen to be a creative process elaborating and maintaining order out of the random-

ness of matter . . . endlessly generating new and unexpected structures and properties. . . ." Kenny sighed and kept on reading.

Marvin led Annalisa around the corner of the house, past a flower bed filled with poppies and lilies, then down a path to a group of people seated around a stone pool. There were two decorators, an architect and his protégé, a young man of about nineteen, Marvin, and Marvin's roommate, David, who was wearing lavender and taupe. They were drinking wine and eating sandwiches and pâté, laughing at everything anyone said. Every now and then one of them would break into hysterical laughter. One by one they would disappear into the house, stay awhile, then return in an even better mood. Down the rabbit hole, Annalisa thought. Well, queers are really very nice. They make everything so pretty. If they wouldn't buttfuck each other they'd be perfect.

"Tell me about the Jesuits," she said to Marvin during a lull in the laughter. "I'm thinking of writing a piece about the order. Do you mind talking about it?"

"Oh, I wasn't a Jesuit, Duckie. I was a Christian Brother. There isn't much to tell. I thought I had a calling and they shipped me off to Arizona and I started having epileptic fits and the brothers told me it was the Holy Ghost filling me up with himself. Charming, what? Finally they decided it was dangerous to keep me so they sent me home. I was seventeen when they decided not to keep me. Dreary, dreary. I wouldn't bother to write about that if I was you. No one wants to read about those dullies. Well, tell us about yourself. Tell about the South."

Then Annalisa drank too much wine and regaled them with tales of the spiritual life of Mobile, Alabama and the

Alabama Gulf Coast. "God's big down there. They have bumper stickers with religious motifs and billboards with pictures of Jesus and many radio stations and TV. There's big money in religion in the South. Fortunes are being made. Of course, it's all incredibly sexy. All those dressed-up ladies in high heels trooping into the Baptist churches every Sunday with their old football players. People singing together in the choir. You can smell the musk." The group broke into peals of laughter. "There's really nothing like it up here. I mean, up here everything seems so Hegelian, I don't get the feeling of anything sensual going on, except occasionally a sort of thwarted sexuality at the Roman Catholic mass."

"I envy you that material," Marvin said. "Oh, I've got to go down there and visit. The football players are at the Baptist church? That's where you find them? Well, we've just got to see each other more often. I know what. Let's start a round table at the Russian Tea Room. Yes, on Wednesdays. Oh, say you'll come, starting this week." Annalisa giggled and had another glass of wine. One of Marvin's guests started describing a flower clock made of all the flowers that open and close at certain times of the day. The afternoon wore on. Kenny had given up on the book and gone in the kitchen to have some tea. At five o'clock Annalisa drank one last glass of Piesporter Goldtröpfchen, estate bottled, mies in cabernet, and they drove back down the line of elms. She was cuddled up in the backseat babbling on about Marvin and his friends and what a good time she'd had.

"A bunch of queers doing coke," Kenny said. "That's how you're going to spend your time from now on?"

"They are very nice people. Mr. Fannin is arranging for the two of us to go on the Phil Donahue show. And I would ask you to show a little Christian charity, not to mention broadmindedness and lack of prejudice where other people's intimate lives are concerned. We are not on this earth to cast stones at glass windows, lest the house we break might be our own. I'm getting sleepy. Oh, I should never drink wine in the daytime. I should not do it."

"Don't go on TV with that little queer. Look at them dogs. What kind of man would keep them dogs. I wouldn't trust that Marvin Fannin to hand me an aspirin, much less get me on a talk show."

"Well, I don't care to discuss it anymore. I am worn out and I'm going to sleep."

"What's your editor going to say when he finds out you been out drinking wi.h the competition and told him you'd go on Phil Donahue without even checking with the paper first? You got to remember who you are, Annalisa. . . ." But she was fast asleep, with her legs drawn up against her stomach. She looked so sweet Kenny wanted to stop the car and just look at her. She is some kind of woman, he was thinking. She has turned me around in the department of trusting white people and I am not letting any little wiggle-ass queer take advantage of her. That is that. He took her sweater and laid it across her legs and drove on back to the city.

Perhaps she felt his hand touch her legs as he covered her. Perhaps she was sleeping in a sea of his concern. Perhaps she was terrified of what she was becoming. Whatever caused it, as she rocked along in the backseat of the cab, Annalisa began to have a very lifelike dream.

She and Kenny arrived in the city after dark. They went up to her apartment on the elevator. She was still half-asleep. She was leaning on his arm.

"You want me to pick you up tomorrow?" he said at the door.

"Come on in, and let me look at my book."

"We got that pray-in in the afternoon. Don't forget that."

"Oh, God, I'd forgotten." She paraded barefoot into the living room and threw herself down on the couch. "I am thirty-six years old, Kenny. And I do not even have a baby. Get us a Coke out of the refrigerator, will you?"

"It's from hanging out with queers. They'll do it to you."

"Don't say that anymore. We have to be kind, Kenny. We have to love each other or perish. Queers are no worse than other people, everyone has to have someone to love. I'll admit I wish they wouldn't buttfuck each other but heterosexual men sometimes abuse people too and women do mean things. Oh, I give up. Some days I give up."

"Here's your Coke." She took it from him and motioned him to a chair beside her. "It is nineteen eighty-four. Man is holding on by his fingernails to his fragile hard-won illusion of civilization. I am weary of the fray, Kenny. I do not take the pill but I am equipped with a diaphragm that has not failed me yet and if you would like to sleep with me I will go and put it on."

"I'm game if you are."

"Take me to the bedroom," she said. "Have your way with me."

She woke up as they were pulling into the midtown tunnel. A woman psychiatrist was on the radio talking about screen memories. Kenny turned down the volume when he saw she was awake. "My first memory," he began, "is of my Aunt Mystina always letting me fool around when we hung up the wash. She was so loose, she didn't care what any-

body did. We used to make parachutes out of the sheets. I
have always wanted to go skydiving because of that. I have
this friend out in New Jersey that runs a skydiving school. I
am planning on going back to school to study engineering
so I can design planes and special parachutes for diving.
There should be other uses for flight except dropping
bombs on people and carrying lawyers around from one
town to another. When man said, I wish I could fly, he
didn't mean to go dropping bombs on anybody. No, what
he wanted was to fly like a bird. Well, that's my secret
dream. Now I've told it to you."

"My first memory," she said, shaking herself awake, "is
falling off a sofa with a bottle in my mouth. Kenny, do you
think of me as an old maid? I mean, be honest. Do you?"

"No, but I think you have gone crazy if you go on Phil
Donahue with that queer."

"I don't want you to say queer anymore in front of me."

"Well, here we are. You want me to come and get you in
the morning?"

"Let's don't argue. I value this friendship deeply, Kenny.
I was thinking this morning about that day we went to the
Van Gogh exhibition and ate that cornbread. Yes, I do
want you to come get me in the morning. See you then."
She got out, having managed to get in the last word, which
was not easy with Kenny. She pushed through the revolv-
ing doors of her building and marched across the foyer.

"You okay?" The elevator boy said. He was a big fan of
Annalisa's and bragged to everyone that he knew her.

"I'm fine."

"You look depressed."

"Well, I'm not. I'm perfectly okay."

* * *

Then two weeks went by while Annalisa prepared for the Phil Donahue show. She and Marvin were expected to argue their different approaches to church criticism, Marvin taking the position that all one had to do was be a good reporter. "I'll show you horse thieves, you tell me if horse thieves are evil," was Marvin's motto. Annalisa was supposed to defend a more subjective view.

"You can do this if you want to," her editor said. "But for God's sake don't implicate the paper or state positions for the *Times*. Make it clear that you are speaking as an individual. And be careful about getting excited. They can zoom in and make you look crazy."

"I don't believe you're going through with it," Kenny said. "That Phil Donahue is the most stuck-up guy on TV He's so full of himself. He don't care what he says to anybody. Hasn't got any manners. What you doing this for?"

"Then don't drive me. Send somebody else."

"I'll drive you. What time we got to go?"

"We need to leave at six. We go on at nine."

"I'll be there."

"Thank you."

All night the night before the progam she lay in bed thinking of things to say and not say. She imagined the camera zooming in on her eyes. Madness would be written there. She woke in a sweat several times and went into the bathroom and examined her face in the mirror. Yes, the camera would seek her out and know her. She would be laid bare before the whole United States. It would be all over, the small fame of which she had been so proud would be shattered by the cold light of the TV.

Not only that, but her faith, which lately had been wavering like a candle in the wind, would be shown up for the tattered thing it was. Do you believe in what you're doing? The accusers would rise up around her like Valkyries. Do you believe in anything?

No, Annalisa would answer and they would ring down the curtain on her career.

Kenny got her to the studio an hour before the show began. It was a building near the river. A stone bully, Annalisa thought. Which will swallow me and spit me out. Oh, well.

"You want me to go up with you?" Kenny said.

"Sure. You can watch it on the monitor."

"If I can stand to."

"Well, that's all I need right now, as nervous as I am, for you to talk like that. Come on, let's go." They pushed through the glass doors to the reception room. No one seemed to know who she was, or to care. It was many minutes before a boy appeared to lead her to a dressing room. There was another long wait. Then a makeup lady appeared and began to work on her face. Finally, Phil came in, talking over his shoulder to a woman holding a clipboard. "Well, I guess you're all ready to go," he said.

"Is Mr. Fannin here yet? He said he'd meet me here at seven."

"He'll be along. You can look over this list of questions we might ask, if you'd like."

"Sure. Hand them here." Phil handed her the clipboard and smiled. "We've had a lot of requests for you," he said. "You have quite a following out there."

"I might not have after this morning."

"Oh, I wouldn't think like that," he said. Then Marvin

appeared at the door. "Well, I'm just nervousness's old auntie Maud. Aren't you dying, angel? I haven't slept a minute."

"Neither have I. I don't know why we thought this up. Why are we doing this, Marvin?"

"Publicity, precious. You can't buy this kind of exposure."

"I don't want to buy it. I have a job working for the world's best newspaper. Why am I going on this TV show?"

"Well, you don't have a thing to worry about, angel. We're going to make you look so good. When we get through there'll be agents all over the place begging to sign you up."

"I don't want to sign up for anything. Kenny, this man that drives me. He said he thought . . ." A bell went off. The makeup lady added two strokes of rouge. The clipboard lady led them to the sound stage.

Kenny was watching it in the lounge, sitting on the edge of his chair, holding a Styrofoam cup of lukewarm coffee in his hand. The logo came on. Phil walked out into the audience and began charming the ladies. He walked among a carpet of permanent waves, smiling and laughing. Credits rolled. An advertisement for furniture polish, being sold by a sweet-looking old man. He tapped a nail into an antique chair, rubbed it with polish. A canoe shot down a river and came to rest on a beach. A man and a woman in hiking clothes ran into the woods and lifted a coffeepot from a fire. They drank and pronounced it good. The logo again. Then Phil was on the stage talking about Annalisa. "One critic said she is a virus visited upon the spiritual life of the city. Buckley loves her. The archbishop refuses to comment, and here to talk about the new field of church criticism is Miss

Annalisa Livingston herself, Our Lady in Your Pew."
There was desultory applause. Kenny sighed and finished
off the coffee.

"Well, Annalisa," Phil was saying. "We're hoping you'll
tell us about how you got started writing church criticism.
What motivated you? You were at *Woman's World* for a
while, weren't you? As an editor?"

"Well, yes, I was there for six years. I liked it there. I just
thought this other idea up, this column, and then the *Times*
thought it was good so we just took off." She giggled. "We
never thought all this would happen."

"You're being given quite a bit of freedom, aren't you? I
can't believe the things they're letting you get away with
over there."

"Get away with? What are you talking about?"

"I mean, criticizing ministers' private lives and making
jokes about sermons. It's not something you see in the *New
York Times* too often."

"I am doing my work. It's just like covering the theater or
reviewing books. It's not reporting." She was getting edgy.
From the place where he was watching the monitor Kenny
sighed and rubbed his hands together. Don't get mad, he
was thinking. Stay cool.

"So you decided that you'd stop being an editor and take
up writing. Is that it? I mean, did you have any formal
training in religion or religious studies? Anything like
that?"

"I didn't need any. I know how to write. Any intelligent
person who can read can write. Churches are the repository
of a culture's spiritual ideals. They must be kept strong.
That's what all the reformations have been about."

"Oh, so you think of yourself as a sort of one-woman ref-
ormation?"

"I didn't say that. You said that."

"I'm sorry."

"Ask him some questions. It's his turn." She was getting mad now. She didn't like anything about this show. She didn't like Phil and she didn't like his suit and she hated the ladies with their hairdos and she was beginning to hate Marvin for looking so pleased and smug. "It's your turn, Marvin. You thought this up. You talk."

"Her father was a minister," Marvin said. "Tell them about your childhood, Annalisa. Tell them about being the preacher's child."

"What is this?" she said. "What's going on here?" The camera took that moment to move in. The lights were in her eyes. The ladies were leaning toward the stage.

"Her father was an Episcopal priest. Isn't that true, Annalisa?"

"Well, yes, he was."

"Is he still living?"

"Yes, thank God."

"But he's no longer in the church?"

"Where did you find that out? Who have you been talking to?" She was leaning forward. Don't break, Kenny was thinking. He was standing up. Marvin was putting a briefcase on his lap. Looking for something as he talked. "Your father got into some kind of trouble with the church, didn't he? Some problem in Kentucky?"

"What are you talking about?" She was on her feet. "How dare you?"

"We all know how those things go," Marvin said. "People are only human, after all. A little scandal never — "

"Oh, I say, that's too much. Let's settle down around here," Phil had his hand on Marvin's arm but it was too late. "Allegations," she was screaming. "Allegations and

lies. Lies and false witness . . . dirty lies. . . ." Marvin pulled
a yellowed newspaper out of a briefcase and spread it on his
lap.

"It says here," he began. "The Reverend William Livingston of Saint Mark's Episcopal Church . . ." Annalisa
was on him now. She had the paper in her hands. "My
sainted father," she was screaming. "A pure saint if one
ever lived. You little queer, how dare you say his name, his
precious name. . . ." Phil was beside her. He had his arms
around her waist. The audience was going wild. A river appeared on the screen.

"I'll sue everybody on this stage," Annalisa was saying.
"I'll sue this goddamn studio for a million dollars. Get me
out of here." She turned to the audience. "There are people starving in the world. Haven't any of you got anything
better than this to do?" She stalked past the cameras and
the technicians and found her pocketbook in the dressing
room and headed down the hall. A man in a sport shirt
tried to stop her. She hit at him with her bag. "Get out of
my goddamn way, you goddamn television wart, who
would work for anything this inane. Get out of my way."
Then she was in the waiting room. Kenny was standing by
the door. "Let's go," she said. "And don't you dare say I
told you so."

They went down the elevator and across the marble floor
and out the glass doors into the light. The sun was shining
on the river. The sun was shining on Kenny's cab.

"I want to sit up front with you," she said.

"It's fine with me. Push that cigar box on the floor. I
don't know about you, Annalisa, but I'm starving. I know
this place where we can get some oysters. This guy from

New Orleans runs it. Fried oysters and French bread. You did good, Annalisa. Time somebody told him off. Everyone in town will be glad you did it, so stop thinking about the Phil Donahue show and let's get something to eat."

"Afterwards," she said, "I would like to have you come over to my apartment."

"Well, I knew this was going to happen." He turned around to her on the seat. "Don't start something with me unless you mean it. I am a man and I have been having feelings about you for some time now."

"I mean it." Annalisa reached over and put her small blue-veined hand on his leg at the place where the long muscle joins the knee. On the sidewalk behind them an Irishman left the war that was raging in his head against the British and started one against a tribe in Africa. A girl on her way home from an all-night job in a bakery had a thrill of envy at the sight of a good-looking black man leaning over a white woman. The Milky Way moved above them in the spring sky. A comet that was not scheduled to appear for six months sailed in their direction. Annalisa lifted her face and waited for a kiss. Kenny decided to let her wait. "This is going to make our business relationship a lot of trouble. I am a man. Be sure you want this before you start it with me."

"You have already told me that. Now, where's this place that has oysters for breakfast?"

"Out in Brooklyn. They got a jukebox with James Booker and Doctor John and Trane and Little Stevie. Moise puts the records in himself. It's not some jukebox owned by the Mafia like most of them around here." Kenny pulled out into the traffic and started driving to Brooklyn. Annalisa moved closer to him, but not too close. She was taking it slow. "This is how love affairs often start,

Kenny. Two people run into each other in the normal course of their lives. It is not true that we fall in love on some enchanted evening at some cocktail party when we are all dressed up. It is better and more normal and healthier for it to happen this way."

"There's a lot going on everywhere lately. That book you gave me, about the chains of illusion. I've been reading that. It says all we are is this big pile of stuff that keeps on making new things out of itself. This same stuff that has always been here just keeps making something new, each thing crazier than the last. Do you believe that?"

"Today I believe anything. I'm quitting this job, Kenny. I'm not writing down what I think anymore for anyone to see or talk about or criticize. To hell with them. Love you one day, hate you the next. I'm going to work for a bank or a shoe store."

"You'll change your mind. You just burned out and mad. Need something to eat. You're thin as a rail."

"Can we dance at this oyster place? I think I feel like dancing."

"I already told you it's the best jukebox in town."

"Good. Imagine that little bastard digging up that paper on my father. It was just a nasty story in a paper. It wasn't even true." She moved closer, thinking how long the bones were in his legs, thinking maybe she would get a loft in SoHo and decorate it Japanese and have Kenny move in. Change the course of her life. Move in with Kenny and quit the *Times*. That would show them. Let them talk about that on their nasty Yankee television shows.

"We are going to be the talk of the town," she said, and slid even closer still.

Next thing I know she'll be wanting to get married,

Kenny thought. These white women go crazy if you make them come.

Annalisa moved her hand farther up his leg. The taxi lurched out onto the Brooklyn Bridge. The comet burned and held its course. In a band of stars a billion light-years long this was not the only important thing going on. But it was one of them.

The Last Diet

ON THE TWENTY-FOURTH DAY OF AUGUST, nineteen hundred and eighty-five, JeanAnne Lori Mayfield, third child and only daughter of Mr. and Mrs. Johnny Wayne Mayfield of Fayetteville, Arkansas, ended her last and final diet by running her navy blue Toyota sedan into a doughnut shop. She could have swerved the other way and hit the emergency entrance of the Washington County General Hospital, but, no, she plowed into the front window of Daytime Doughnuts, Number Three, killing a waitress, an overweight professor of English at the university and herself. Goodbye, JeanAnne Lori, we will miss you. Goodbye, Aurora Gilbreath. We'll miss you too. Goodbye, Professor Bright. Wasn't it you who always used to say, "When you're hungry, eat; when you're sleepy, sleep. Pass the cornbread."

Once, when he was younger, Professor Bright had been

married to a redhaired graduate student who had borne him a son. A thin, redheaded boy named Teddy who loved books and who had spent his life, up to the time of the crash at Daytime Doughnuts, reading anything he could get his hands on. He was reading a book when the phone rang to tell him of the tragedy. He closed the book, laid it on a table and hurried to the hospital to identify the body.

The worst thing of all for Teddy Bright was that he knew everyone involved. He knew his father and lived down the street from him. He knew Aurora Gilbreath and had purchased doughnuts from her many a morning on his way to work. He knew JeanAnne Lori and had been in the room with her many times, at restaurants around town, or at the Kinko's Copy Place where she worked. Teddy even knew where JeanAnne Lori lived.

She lived across the street from the park, in a small white house facing a castle built by a local sculptor with a National Endowment Grant. It was a castle made of concrete and stone, of rocks and mussel shells, of old earrings and clay tiles with strange runes engraved on them. The castle was used as an example of how grant money is wasted on useless projects, but no one tore it down, and never a day went by that there wasn't a meeting between lovers or a picnic or a birthday party taking place on its turrets and battlements and towers. JeanAnne Lori's house faced the castle and Teddy had delivered many a pizza to her door during the years when he was working his way through college. It would be a Combination Deep-Dish or an International or a Madrid.

Now, here was Teddy, standing in JeanAnne Lori's yard, trying to believe his father was dead. He hung his head. It could not be true. His father stretched out on an undertaker's table. JeanAnne Lori, dead and to blame. There was her house, being sat in by her friends. He went inside, and was comforted and given a glass of tea.

"Would you like to see her room?" her friend Stella said. "She left everything in perfect order." Teddy was led back through a narrow hall to JeanAnne Lori's room. A spotless white rug was on the floor. A white coverlet with puffs of pink cotton was on the bed. Pillows with pink and white shams. Five Care Bears lined up on the pillows. Share Bear, Cheer Bear, Friend Bear, Good Luck Bear, Brave Heart Bear. A white enamel table held JeanAnne Lori's Bible and her diary and a vase of artificial flowers. Teddy picked up the Bible. "I'll leave you here to meditate," Stella said. As soon as she was gone Teddy put the Bible down and picked up the diary and put it in his pocket. Then he walked back down the hall and told Stella goodbye and went across the street to the castle and up a path to a turret room that looked out on the baseball diamond. He opened the book and began to read.

A DIET JOURNAL, by J. L. Mayfield, age 38

I begin this diet as no other diet. This time I will win. This time I will not be tempted by anything to stop short of my goal. It took a long time to gain this weight. It is going to take a long time to lose it. Now, get up, weigh myself. Go on. I gained it. Now I must pay.

Later: 148. Oh, my God!

APRIL 2, 1985
Five glasses of water — all vitamins — some lettuce and egg white, some diet rice cakes — three or four — I can't re-

member exactly. One chicken breast. No. I will not eat another bite all day. I will lie down and imagine myself very very very thin. I am wearing a soft white dress and leaning on somebody's arm. He is going to take me to the show I think. I will drink one Diet Coke — that is absolutely all.

APRIL 3
Today is the day I will have to really think straight and everything. My body is resisting being hungry. The body is not on your side in anything. Sex or diet. I must always keep that first in my mind above all other things and defeat it with my mind. The mind is stronger than the body if it wants to be.

APRIL 4
I will not get down or mad at myself if I slip and eat one cookie or even a milk shake in a moment of weakness. I will never see my waist again unless I start right now. I will be in a sea of fat. It will surround my natural beauty like a lake. So there is nothing to do now but charge ahead.

Think of all that fat around my heart and liver if I should ever have to get an operation. Of course, so far I have been in perfect health all my life, but you never can tell. Yes, I think I am on my way to a body any woman could be proud of. Yes, this time I will win at the losing game.

Later: I have had a strange spell of weakness. It was the first time I ever felt weak in my life. I could not get up off the floor. I called the Weight Engineers and they said not to worry it is only my body wanting some food. I will drink some more water and lay on the floor and wait it out.

JUNE 18
Dear Diet Diary, I have not been writing in you because I have been in the hospital. I drained all the potassium out of my body and had an electrolyte imbalance. I am sorry that

happened as it was a major diet setback and I have gained
back all the weight I lost that wonderful week of starvation
and now I have to start all over again. The Weight Engineers said not to get excited about it, that doctors always
want to blame things on women starving themselves when
that wasn't it at all. It was the heat and the long sunbaths I
was taking to give myself something to do while I was
starving. I have to go back to work tomorrow so it will not
be easy to diet properly at the store, but I will make it one
way or the other.

JUNE 19
First I have to get out all my clothes and lay them on the
bed and pick out something beautiful I want to wear on the
first of September. By the first of September I will be a size
8 or die. That is absolutely that. I have had it with being the
size of a house. I want a new boyfriend and a good social life
and I will never get it until I conquer the layers of fat that
have come like a terrible parasite to nest on my rib cage and
my hips and my arms. I must be very clear about my goals
now.
1. My goal is to be a size 8 by September 1.
2. My immediate goal is to be a size 12 by the first of August. This means I have to be a person who can live on 700
calories a day and not complain.
    I must think of a lot of interesting things to do around
town and not forget to let my friends help me. They may be
secretly jealous when they see my rib cage and slim hips
emerging from the mountain of fat cells that hold them
captive. Let them be jealous. That's their problem.

JUNE 27
My adviser at Weight Engineers say that I am the best
dieter (diet student) they have had. I don't give up just because I have a few setbacks. I know what I want and I will

make the sacrifices to get it. They are going to give me a free week's counseling to make up for having to go to the hospital.

When I have reached my goal of 125 pounds, then I will make a video tape for them about how I did it and they can play it for other people. It feels so good to be on my way to success in the diet field.

I would a lot rather be skinny than go get some sweet rolls for breakfast. Look at it this way, sweet rolls are just going to last a few minutes. A good body will be with me always.

Teddy looked up. Some children were playing on the castle. They were on the bridge, dropping rocks into the moat. A girl caught his eye, then reached down and scratched her behind. She was a dirty wild-looking fat little blond girl. Teddy decided he loved her. I hope when you grow up you never think you are fat, he was thinking. I hope you never hear the word. He turned the page of the diary. From August 3 to August 14 was blank. August 14 was written in sharp black printing, as if the writer were leaning the weight of the universe against the pen.

AUGUST 14

I begin again. Nothing to lose but my self-esteem completely if I don't. I have been driving down Mission Road so my car would never go by the shopping center where they have my darling angel Weight Engineers, who have helped me so much. Why did I give up short of goal? Just because my potassium got low and I got sick *one* day and my arm was a little bit numb. Is that any reason to give up the only diet I ever went on that was going to be successful? It was successful. I still am twelve pounds below where I started in April. I have lost twelve pounds forever and I will lose ten more. I weigh 136 and my goal is 125 and I will get there. I am in control again. I am so happy. I sat over on the castle

this morning and thought about Frank Williams, who built
it with his own hands when he lived here. I used to see his
old truck pull up full of stones. Now this monument to him
is here forever. My diet will be like that. A few stones to
carry each day, then my castle will stand there before my
eyes. My body will be perfect as God and nature intended it
to be.

Teddy sighed. It was too sad. The world was just too
much to bear. He lay his head against the tiles in the turret
wall. Heavenly music began to play. Heavenly music coming for to carry him home. He looked up. It was the ice
cream truck turning the corner by the swimming pool. A
red and white striped truck with a carousel on top. The
horses on the carousel were freshly painted. They whirled
around and around as the truck moved down the hill playing Strauss waltzes to a calliope beat. The children left the
bridge and ran to the corner to watch it go by. Teddy went
back to JeanAnne Lori's diary.

AUGUST 15
I have just purchased a set of doctor's scales. They take up
half my bathroom. I dreamed of them last night. I am not
sleeping very well without food but it's all right. When I
wake up I walk around the house and think about how good
I'm going to look. It won't be long now. Twenty more days
of hunger and it will all be over.
      Later: Some headaches this afternoon, nothing special.
Took some aspirin and a Tylenol I borrowed from Angela
Jamesison. You have to put up with a few inconveniences.
Also, foot getting numb when I set in one position for more
than a few minutes. Nothing to worry about.

AUGUST 16
I bought a diet placemat at the health food store. It has 33
different diets and six fasts. It is great. Just reading it makes

me know it is possible to get thin if I want to enough and
don't get sidetracked and think I have to be thin to get a
boyfriend. The point of getting thin is for my own self-
esteem and to love myself and so forth.

It is the wrong approach to a diet to think that at the end
you will have some wonderful boyfriend who will change
the world. Monique, my weight counselor, says that is the
thing that makes everyone gain back weight after they
struggled so hard to lose it. They get thin, then nothing
happens in the romance department, so they give up and go
back to eating. That will not happen to me because I know
about it beforehand.

The placemat cost $4.98 and is copyrighted so you can't
tell the diets to anyone without permission. There is one
that gives you six animal crackers for a reward every night.
That goes along with something Monique was telling me.
She said the body will not live without pleasure. So you
have to be very good to yourself while you are starving and
have other pleasures like making your yard beautiful or
getting a new shower curtain. Or talking to your friends.

AUGUST 17

I am nearing my goal. Yesterday my arm got numb again
while I was cleaning out a closet. I think I might be catch-
ing something. I keep having this light get in my eye. I don't
want to say anything about it because they might make me
stop the diet. I need the diet. The diet is the best thing that
ever happened to me. Before I went on the diet I didn't
know who I was. I didn't have a sense of purpose. I just got
up in the morning and went to work and came home. I
could not plan a future for myself. Well, nothing will stop
me now.

The people at Weight Engineers have made me Dieter of
the Month. I am going to have my picture in their newslet-
ter and maybe in the national Weight Engineers' magazine.
It is a good thing I am keeping this diary. I think there will

come a time when it will be a very important document. Well, that's about all for now. I have to eat lunch and then go get weighed in. Oh, yes, every day as I turn off the highway to go to the Weight Engineers office I have to pass right by the doughnut shop. It is wonderful to see fat people going in to get their sugar and caffeine fix when I know that I am on my way to clearer goals and better thinking.

AUGUST 19

I have had a setback caused by listening to the radio. There was this woman from Georgia and she said she and her friends had started a club called Bored Of The Fat and every time one of them decided to go on a diet or spend money on diet camps or diet food or anything like that they called a meeting and sat down with a box of cookies and some Häagen Dazs ice cream and reminded each other of how beautiful the world is and how much fun it is to eat things.

They shouldn't put things like that on the air. I went right down to the grocery and pigged out. It was all that woman's fault. I am going to write the station. Now, I must call Monique and get back in control. I will get back in control. I will be in control.

AUGUST 20

What next? I shouldn't even write this down but I saw Josephine Wethers today and she looked like hell. She has been going to Diet Jail, as we call Weight Engineers for a joke, for four months now and at first she looked real good, but now she looks like a person who went to Dachau or something. I was shocked when I ran into her. All the way home I kept thinking I might be thin enough already and not know it. I weigh 128, the least I have ever weighed except when I had pneumonia. I don't know what to think or do sometimes. All the way home I kept thinking about how thin and gaunt her face looked. What if I look like that and no one tells me? I wouldn't have told her for anything. Imagine me walking up to her and saying, Josephine, you look terrible.

Exercise, that's the key. Maybe I should start running again. But all it does is make me hungrier and hungrier. I know it's muscle weight, but it still depresses me to see it on those damn old scales.

Maybe I should throw the scales away. Oh, no, never say that. They are only science, remember Monique said they are only the measurement of what we are attempting to do. Oh, God, I'll always be fat. I can't defeat it. I don't know what to do.

Later: I am in control. I went to Weight Engineers and talked to Monique and she said it was just a temporary setback and to forget the milk shake I drank last night and the cheese and crackers and think about the future when I will be a size 8 and ready for romance. I don't know where that's going to be in Fayetteville. Maybe there's somewhere to go in Rogers.

AUGUST 21

I have failed again. Last night I ate two Lean Cuisines and half a pound of Weight Engineers Rye Thins. I gained another pound. Now I am back up to 129 and only two days ago I was 127. I was two pounds from my goal and I messed it up by being weak. I remind myself of my mother. That is what she would do when she was mad. Just eat another bag of potato chips and give some to me. Not to mention ice cream cones. There is no hope for me. I have tried everything but having my intestines shortened by surgery. I need to get my mind on something besides myself. There must be something to cheer me up.

Wait a minute! This is my Weight Diary. No place to feel sorry for myself. I must get hold of myself. Drink eight glasses of water. And some lemon juice and parsley. I will get this under control if it's the last thing I ever do in my life.

AUGUST 23

I have started a fast. For fourteen hours I have not had a thing to eat but water and four ounces of orange juice. I will write in this book every hour until I weigh 125. Where I really want to be.

12:00   Water
 1:00   Water
 1:35   Going to bed
 3:15   Can't sleep
 4:00   Took one of the Demerols I saved when Mama was sick.
 9:40   Good sleep. Drank two eight-ounce glasses of water.
12:00   Four ounces of orange juice. I'm feeling weak but that's to be expected the first day. Will meditate.
 8:00   Walked five miles, drank water, swam 18 laps. Drank four ounces of orange juice.
10:00   Going to bed.
11:35   Can't sleep.
 3:00   Still can't sleep. Have cleaned the whole house. Will take the other Demerol.

AUGUST 24, 6:00 A.M.

I am into a wonderful state of fast now. I am very clear. I remember when I took that class in Zen Buddhist scriptures from Doctor Bright at the university and he told us about the states the enlightened men would go into from not eating sometimes for days. I think I might be getting into one of those. I feel like something real important is happening to me. Like I am in the middle of real important events. It is like falling in love or when my niece, Lori Louise, was born and I rode around all night on my bicycle because Sally and Jimmy had named her for me. I think I should be a painter and paint all the glorious things I have been seeing on my fast. There is one small problem.

I have had a headache but took some aspirin and also my right arm got numb, but it is fine now. Also, I could not see to read. The brain is a funny thing and will have to adjust to this new state of affairs. 125. Here I come.

Idea. As soon as the stores open I will go out to the mall and look at all the beautiful clothes I will be buying as soon as I am at goal. I called Monique and she said to come by and let her monitor me since fasting is not a regular part of Weight Engineers diets and she is only letting me do it because I am frantic.

Well, sayonara for now.

The rest of the pages were blank. Teddy closed the book. The children had come to the moat below the turret and were fishing for crawdads. A boy came running out from inside the dungeon. He had a huge crawdad between the thumb and index finger of his right hand and he was holding it out toward the little blond girl. She began to scream, a wonderful bloodcurdling scream. The boy laughed and withdrew the crawdad. The girl screamed some more.

A van pulled into the parking lot and unloaded a Little League baseball team. Music was playing in the background. The ice cream truck was circling back around. Teddy took two one-dollar bills out of his pocket and laid them on a bench beside the moat. "Here's some money," he said. "Go over there and get some ice cream when I'm gone. It's all right. I'm only putting this here because I'm sad." The children backed off. "It's all right to take the money when I'm gone," he added. He left the money on the bench and walked back across the street in the direction of Jean-Anne Lori's house. I have to decide what to do about everything now, he was thinking. I have to make decisions. He looked around. There was a trash container beside an elm tree. He dropped the diary in and walked back to his car.

Behind him the little girl picked up the money from the bench and began to run in the direction of the painted horses on the painted truck.

III
The Islands

The Blue-Eyed Buddhist

SALLY LANIER SYKES was going to die. There was no getting around that. She was thirty-four years old and she
could count on the fingers of one hand the years she had
left to sail the British Virgin Islands or dance all night at
parties or roll up her hair or paint her toenails or worry
about dying.

Sally Sykes only had one kidney and that one used to belong to her daddy and as soon as she got back to Guntersville, Georgia she was going to have to trade it in for a
machine. Needless to say, she was having a hard time getting used to the idea. . . .

Not that Sally Sykes was going to have to go to a hospital
and get hooked up with a lot of boring sick people. Back in
Guntersville an architect and a builder and a decorator

and four carpenters were working right this minute to build her a room so beautiful no one would ever imagine anything unpleasant could go on in it. In the meantime all she had to do was lie on the deck of the sailboat tanning the backs of her legs and brood about turning loose the sharks in the research station at The Bitter End. The sharks and the manta ray and the puffer fish and the turtles and the angels.

"I am going to do it," she said to herself. "By God, I am going to do it." Among other things it would make a nice addition to her memoirs. Sally was spending the summer writing on her memoirs.

I was born into a world so polite that no one ever told the truth about anything, she wrote, *and into a religion so advanced its members were even spared the discomfort of dying.* Dying, dying, dying. Dead as a doornail. Done. No more rain, no more nothing. No possum, no sop, no taters.

She looked down at what she had written. Several drops of Germaine Monteil dark tanning oil ran down her nose and onto the paper, forming a little lake right in the middle of the page. More drops fell. A little river of oil and perspiration running down the page and onto the mahogany deck of the sailboat. The sailboat was anchored in the middle of paradise. A small cove behind the airport on the island of Tortola in the British Virgin Islands. It was late June, a clear still morning, a paradisal day in paradise. As far as the eye could see, north, east, south, west, up or down, right or left, underwater or above it was paradise. Air the color of turquoise, water, a million jeweled shades of blue. Air so clean you could drink it, Sally thought. If I drank that air I would be well. There wouldn't be any old filthy blood that needed cleaning. Dirty blood, that's what I'm going to die of. Dirty blood, sounds like a rock song.

Perfumed sweat rolled down upon the memoirs. Sally's heart beat like a drum. Her father's old right kidney strained to live.

I could always ask him for the other one, she thought. He would probably give it to me.

"Sally," Malcolm called from the cabin. Malcolm was her husband. "Come down here a minute. Come help me pack."

She got up from the deck and stretched her arms over her head. She was wearing only the bottom half of a very small emerald bikini and no one looking at her would imagine she had ever been sick a day in her life.

She reached down into the cockpit and stuck an old Bob Dylan tape into the tape player. *Hey, Mr. Tambourine Man, play a song for me,* he was singing. *In your jingle-jangle morning I'll come following you.*

"Sally," Malcolm called again. "Please come on down here." He stuck his head up through the entrance to the galley. "Are you sure you'll be all right? Are you sure you don't mind me leaving Jimmy here?"

"Of course I'll be all right," she said. "We'll all be fine. Please stop worrying about it."

"I'm not worrying. I could take him with me." They had picked up Malcolm's twelve-year-old nephew at camp and brought him along to the islands. He lived next door to them in Guntersville. They took him with them nearly every year. They pretended he was their own.

"It's fine, Malcolm. It's really fine."

"I don't have to go."

"Of course you have to go. It's only until Thursday."

"I don't know."

"Oh, for God's sake, Malcolm. Please stop all that stuff.

Where have Jimmy and Li gone with the dinghy? You'd better find them and get going or you'll miss the plane."

Malcolm was all the way up the stairs now. He was wearing his crazed look. Except for his height he could have been her twin. Same blue eyes, same golden hair, same perfect nose. He reached out and touched her arm. Oh, shit, she thought, he's going to start crying again.

"You want to make love?" she said. "We've got time."

"I couldn't now."

"We could try. We could lie around on top of each other and see what happens. How about that?" She took a finger and began to draw on his chest, getting suntan oil all over his white shirt.

"Come on, Sally," he said, "don't do that to me. This is my last shirt." The sound of the dinghy motor interrupted them. "And put something on. You really shouldn't go around like that in front of him."

Jimmy came tumbling up onto the boat, holding an old stone gin bottle in his hand. "Look at this," he said. "I found it on the island. Do you think it's valuable? How much do you think it's worth?"

"A lot," Sally said. "That might be worth a hundred dollars. Give it here. Let me see it." She held it up in her hand. "There's no telling who drank this gin. Some pirate might have had it. Now look here, Jimmy, are you going to take your uncle to the airport or not? It's almost ten o'clock. He's going to miss his plane."

"Where's his bag?" Jimmy said. "I'll get his bag. I've got to go back to that island this afternoon, Sally. I've got to see if there're any more."

"We'll see," she said. "We'll talk about it when you get back."

"Well, I have to go back there," he said, and disappeared down the stairs. He was a wild scrawny-looking boy with a head of dark red hair.

"That child is so much like his daddy it makes me believe in reincarnation," Sally said.

"Many people believe in it," Li Moon said. "It's an interesting thing to believe." She had come aboard and was standing beside them with her perfect posture. The two women smiled into each other's eyes. Sally Sykes and Li Moon Cooper adored each other.

"Then I'm coming back as a tree," Sally said. "A great big live oak tree. No, not a live oak. A madrone. A madrone tree."

"You can't do that," Li said. "Once you are human you can only come back as another human being." The women smiled again as if they knew certain things everyone else on earth was too dumb to understand.

Malcolm lit a cigarette and walked to the back of the boat. He hated it when they started that. He hated it when Li Moon sailed with them. He had hated it since the first time she came walking out of The Moorings carrying the tiny little bundle of things she took with her on a charter. He couldn't believe The Moorings had assigned him a woman skipper. Of course, once Sally laid eyes on her she was a permanent fixture. She sailed with them whenever they went to Anegada or down island to the Grenadines or out into the open ocean. In the winter she and Sally kept up an impassioned correspondence, exchanging books and tapes, complimenting each other on how unusual and talented and powerful and brilliant they were.

Jimmy reappeared with the bag. He and Malcolm climbed down off the back of the boat and got into the dinghy. Li handed down a garbage bag full of trash to be taken ashore.

"Don't go to Anegada," Malcolm said.

"Why would I go to Anegada?" Sally said. "You're the one that always wants to go to Anegada. Jimmy, don't forget Li's Hershey Bars."

"I won't forget," Jimmy said. "I've got the list." He started the little seagull motor, letting it idle. Li dropped the dinghy painter into the boat. "Don't take her to Anegada," Malcolm said. "That's an order."

"Don't forget my candy," Li said. They all laughed. Jimmy propped his foot nonchalantly on top of the garbage bag, twisted the gas feed on the handle, and the little boat roared off across the flat surface of the water.

"The dinghy captain," Sally said. "The one and only James William Sykes. When he was only eleven months old he dragged my hair dryer across the floor and plugged it in and started vacuuming the floor. He was born in his own time. Gasoline and power. All we have to do to keep him happy is keep that little motor full."

"What do we have to do to keep *you* happy?" Li said. "What do *you* want to do now?"

"I want to go to The Bitter End and turn them loose."

"You're kidding."

"No I'm not. You don't have to help me if you don't want to. All you have to do is take me there. How many are there now?"

"Three or four nurse sharks and some angels. Last month they had a huge angel they caught on the wall. I'm sure it's dead by now."

"Will you take me?"

"I don't know if we can get there and back by Thursday."

"Don't worry about Thursday."

"Who'll pick him up?"

"We'll call and tell him to wait. Will you take me? Well, will you?"

"All right," Li said. "Get out the charts. Let's go around the islands. The channel's full of powerboats from Puerto Rico. I'm not going to put up with that all the way to Gorda Sound."

They went down to the galley, spread the charts out on the table and began to plot the course.

The Bitter End was a tiny resort at the tip end of the British Virgin Islands chain. The University of Mississippi maintained a station there for the purpose of studying sea kelp. They were trying to find a way to cure cancer with sea kelp. Every year half a dozen beautiful tan graduate students came down to spend a year on an island paradise studying sea kelp. One of the things the students thought up to do to alleviate the paradisal boredom was capturing reef fish and exhibiting them in a pen connected to the land by a pier. Visiting yachtmen could tie their dinghies up to the pier and inspect the fish on their way in to dinner in the evenings.

"The one I really want to get to is the one in Miami," Sally said. "The one with the porpoises." Li put down the triangle. A faraway look came over her face. "I could tell you things about porpoises," she said finally, then looked away.

"Like what? Tell me."

"Not now. It's the wrong time of day."

"I heard they had one here last year and it died."

"They kept it three weeks and watched it die. Everyone was very angry."

* * *

Death, Sally was thinking, looking down at the charts. North, East, South, West. Death beating the door down, like a mummy, like a vampire, like dead leaves, like dead fish. Like that. Just like that.

"We'll stay tonight at Foxy's," Li said, "then go back out in the morning and get there tomorrow afternoon. You aren't watching."

"I'm watching. I heard everything you said." She picked up her coffee cup and rinsed it out in the sink. The noise of the dinghy rose in the air, then came to a stop as it banged into the back of the sailboat. "What's going on?" Jimmy said, swinging himself down the galley ladder. "Here's the candy. Wait till I tell you what I saw."

"Did you tie down the dinghy?" Li said.

"Of course I did," he said. "What do you think I am, a turd or something?"

"Come on, Jimmy," Sally said. "Don't start that. We want you to act like a grown person. We're going to The Bitter End. We're going to turn the fish loose. We're going to do it, honey. We're really going to do it."

"Everyone wants to do it," he said. "I know a lot of people that want to do it."

"So do I," Li said. "But they don't do it."

"So we're going to do it," Sally said. "You and me and Li are going to do it."

Out past Salt Island the dolphins found them. Li saw them first. Far out on the horizon, five or six, diving and playing in the water. She watched for a while before she told the others. "Look out there," she said. "Dolphins."

"That always happens when you're with us," Sally said. "You always make that happen."

"They're good luck," Li said. "They bring luck."

"Should we feed them?" Jimmy said. He was hanging onto the guy wires, leaning out over the safety rail. It was his favorite post when he wasn't at the wheel or standing on the anchor lines. "They didn't come for food," Li said. "They aren't dogs."

The dolphins were near the boat now, swimming alongside the prow. "We might hit them," Jimmy said. "Be careful."

"They won't get hit," Li said. "You couldn't hit them if you tried."

"I'd forgotten the patterns on their backs," Sally said. "I'd forgotten how strong they are."

"I could tell you stories about them," Li said. "Stories no one would believe."

"Tell them," Jimmy said.

"Not now," she said.

They were far out to the north-northwest of Tortola, headed for Great Camanoe. The boat was sailing itself. Li had trimmed the sails, tied down the wheel and gone below to make a cup of tea. Jimmy was sitting behind the wheel eating cookies and reading *The Pearl*. He had promised to finish his summer reading while he was in the islands. This was the worst one he had read so far. Why are they doing this? he kept wondering. How could they be dumb enough to do a thing like that?

Sally was writing on her memoirs. *Lists of Things Aboard the Wind Chime* was the title of her afternoon's work.

Books. *Ragtime, The Naked Ape, The Pleasure Bond, Coming of*

Age in Samoa, The Greening of America, The Sorcerer of Bolinas Reef, An Unfinished Woman, The Hunting Hypothesis, Fire in the Lake, Trout Fishing in America.

Drugs. Seconal, Dilaudid, aspirin, iodine, Dramamine, prednisone, Immuran, amphogel, Mycitracin. (There was a boy at Tulane that kept one seventeen years.) (Tides are an enigma in the islands.) (Exercise caution in anchoring and navigating.) (Water is precious on the ocean.)

Good ideas. The shortwave radio. The Children's Hour. How to tune in to it? The flags, the telltales, diving the wreck, available light, the Nikonos. As I suspected it is always the killed who object to killing. Bully Beef for lunch. Stupid. Dumb. Stupid. Dumb. Why'd I do that? What about lettuce? Water? Bacteria in water? Am I the killed or killing?

"They'll leave us when we turn back in at Jost Van Dyke," Li asked. "They don't gc in the channel anymore. I haven't seen one inside the channel in years."

"Can we eat at Foxy's tonight?" Jimmy asked.

"Everything is wind on a sailboat," Sally said. "How does that sound for the title of a chapter?"

"If Sally wants to," Li said. "I heard Foxy built a new swing on the tree where he sells shirts. Some kind of mechanical swing. You get a free swing if you buy a shirt. I've been wanting to see it."

"I don't care what we do," Sally said. "As long as we get to a hardware store tomorrow morning. Are you sure they'll have what we need on Virgin Gorda?"

"If they don't have it there it won't be anywhere in the islands closer than Saint John's."

"Well, we have to get clippers," Sally said.

"Not clippers. Bolt cutters. If they don't have any at the

store we'll get some from Little Dix. I know a guy at Little Dix that'll get one for us."

"We've got all the diving stuff," Jimmy said. "There're two tanks."

"Well, don't go getting any ideas about diving," Sally said. "I'm the only one that's going diving."

"I know how," he said. "I've done it in the pool a hundred times. I can do it as well as you can."

"Well, you aren't going to do it. Besides, I need you in the dinghy. I need you to stay on top and let the light down. It isn't going to take very long, you know. It's really a simple thing to do."

"Then why hasn't anyone ever done it?" he said.

"I don't know," Sally said. "Maybe because they aren't from Georgia."

They sailed in peace for a while. Li untied the wheel and they headed back into the channel to moor for the night at Trellis Bay. "We know nothing," she said, looking at Sally, who had pulled up a cushion beside her.

"We know how to make this boat," Jimmy said. "We know how to sail it."

"He's got you," Sally said.

"You have a criminal mind," Li said. "You will grow up to be a banker."

"Go put some wine on ice," Sally said. "We'll celebrate."

"You aren't supposed to drink. Uncle Malcolm said you weren't supposed to drink."

"It doesn't hurt me," Sally said. "Unless he's watching. Actually it's very good for me."

"He said it wasn't good for you."

"Nothing is good for me," she said. "Therefore I am free to do anything. Come on, Jimmy. Put some wine in the cooler for your old aunt. And get on the radio and make reservations at Foxy's or there won't be any lobster left. And for God's sake, everyone remember to wear socks. There're sand fleas all over the beach at Foxy's. The last time I was there I got eaten alive. I sat up all night putting gin on my legs."

She's going to get drunk, Li decided. Well, it never takes her long. I'll give it two hours from the time she opens the wine till she passes out.

It took three and a half hours. First there was a bottle of wine on the boat. Then a long diatribe against Republicans on the dinghy ride to Foxy's. Then she bought T-shirts for everyone in Guntersville. Then she bought a conch shell and some coral earrings. Then another bottle of wine. Then the dance.

Just about the time the lobster was put on the table Foxy put a record by Aretha Franklin on the record player. By the third bar of music Sally was out on the dance floor. Foxy's wife, Dreamy Malone, had danced with Sally before. She came out from behind the bar. The two women faced each other across eighteen feet of sand-covered pavement. Sally did her fabulous half-backbend. Dreamy countered with a bump and grind and they met in the middle with their arms in the air. *"Oh, you don't call anymore,"* Aretha was singing. *"I sit alone and sigh." "I'm gonna knock on your door. Tap on your windowpane."* Sally did some steps from an old tap routine. Dreamy countered with a series of pirouettes. Then they really got down to it. Their hands met and parted. They were back to back. Then in each other's arms. *"I'm gonna knock on your door. Tap on your windowpane. Till you come back again. That's all I'm gonna do."*

By the time the record was finished everyone in the bar

was on their feet applauding. Dreamy helped Sally back to her seat. Sally bowed to the audience, took a few bites of her lobster and passed out with her head on Jimmy's lap.

"I'm glad Uncle Malcolm isn't here," he said.

"So am I," Li Moon agreed.

Jimmy was awake before dawn. Sitting on the prow eating a sandwich, washing it down with ginger ale. The boat was anchored in a wide harbor off Trellis Bay. The sea was calm, the flags and telltales barely moving, the dinghy knocking against the prow.

In a distant valley a shack leaned into the hill, a white shack with a red roof. A woman came out the door and walked down to the beach. She leaned over and began to wash a pan out in the ocean. Jimmy could see her breasts moving as she scoured the pan with sand. He stuffed the rest of the sandwich in his mouth and turned his eyes away.

Farther along the shore were a few small houses, a white church with brown shutters and a gray British customs house with a pier for dinghies.

The hatch cover opened and Sally stuck her head out. "Tie that dinghy down, will you?" she said. "I feel horrible. Jesus Christ, I feel bad."

"Remember that Christmas we came down here and they came out and serenaded us with Christmas songs?" he said. "I think this is where we were. I think it was this island."

"It was the Grenadines," Sally said. "Don't you remember? Where we saw the whales. Come on, Jimmy, do something with that dinghy. It's driving me crazy."

She disappeared back down into the cabin making loud theatrical groans. Jimmy went back to the stern and tied down the dinghy. Two black boys appeared on the beach.

They walked down the pier and put their gear into a fishing boat. A cow called from somewhere in the village. The boat took off across the water, the sun broke from above the mountains, a voice was singing in a cabin.

Mustique, he decided. That's the name of it. Where the English princess lives. That's where they sang to us. He was looking up into the rigging, remembering his mother saying the princess liked young boys. He wondered if she would like him. She might hear about him setting the sharks free. She might read about it in the papers. He imagined his picture in the paper and the princess seeing it. Bring that boy over here to me, she would say. I like the way that boy looks. That's the boy that turned the fish loose.

This time tomorrow they'll be free. They'll be swimming off anyplace they want to go. He imagined them in a pack, sea turtles and sharks and angel fish and fat little puffer fish all swimming along like an armada, headed for the open sea.

"We're leaving as soon as we get ready," Li Moon said. She had walked up so quietly he hadn't heard her. "Do you want breakfast before we go?"

"I already had a sandwich. Is she okay?"

"She's okay. She's getting up. She's just excited."

"She almost did it last year. If Uncle Malcolm hadn't gotten the toolbox away from her. She was drunk and he knocked her down on the deck and got it away from her. Then it fell overboard. Uncle Malcolm had to dive for it the next morning. But we still had to pay for some of the tools. He was just trying to keep her from hurting herself."

"We'll do it this time. I can feel it."

"Don't let her get drunk again, okay? Don't let her drink wine."

"That isn't up to me. Or to you."

They looked at each other. Li Moon removed all the expression from her face. Jimmy removed all the expression from his. They almost bowed.

"I could make a sailor out of you," she said.

"All right," Sally yelled from the cabin. "Somebody get ready to lifeguard me. Here I come." She was coming up the hatch wrapped in a towel. She stepped over the lifeline, did a lovely clean dive into the water and swam off into the morning sun. By the time she pulled herself back up on the motor the boat was ready to sail.

"Let's hit it," Li said. "We've got a long day ahead of us."

They sailed out around the southern tip of the island and started toward Virgin Gorda. Li was in a hurry now. She moved from tiller to mainsail to ginny not saying a word, making small precise adjustments to the sails and rudder, not asking for any help, not wanting any.

"What are we going to do?" Jimmy said. "Tell me exactly what we're going to do."

"We'll go in the dinghy sometime in the morning, oh, about three or four. Then you can let the light down in the water while I go down with a tank and cut it open. I looked at it for a long time last year. There's nothing to it. A baby could do it. There are these posts, uprights, about ten feet apart and all I have to do is cut an opening. Then I'll get back in the dinghy and we'll watch them swim away. Li will stay on the *Wind Chime.*"

"You ought to throw the clippers away after you use them. So they won't have any evidence."

"Do you think they'll get my fingerprints and track me down?"

"No, but they might find out and fire Li Moon."

"That's why she's staying on the *Wind Chime.*"

"No, it isn't," Li said. "The reason I'm not going is because I can't swim. And I don't care if they fire me. One
more cruise with a couple of rotten spoiled lawyers' wives
and I'll end up in the jail for murder. The one before you
got here was the end. This whining girl from New Orleans
who cried every morning. I'm not kidding you. She cried.
They're getting worse, and there're too many boats. They
don't know what they're doing. They can kill you."

"You could come and live in Guntersville," Jimmy said.
"We would like to have you there."

The ship's chandler's store on Virgin Gorda had what
they needed. A pair of wire cutters the British proprietor
promised would cut through anything. "You don't need
bolt cutters. This is a nice little tool, actually. Look at these
jaws." He ran his finger along the cutting edge. "What do
you need it for?"

"To cut a chain-link fence?" Sally said.

"Well, be damned careful when you do. That wire's
going to pop when you cut it. They string those things
tight. It'll pop on you if you're not watching."

"Thank you," Sally said. She took the cutters in her
hand. She slipped them into her bag and paid the man.

They sailed through the pass between Gorda Sound and
Mosquito Bay with all sails flying, Jimmy at the helm,
Sally tending the lines, and Li Moon sitting on the hatch
cover filing her fingernails.

"Aren't you even going to watch the sandbars for me?"
he said.

"You know the way," she said. "You went through here last week."

"Well, at least tell me what to do," he said.

"What if you were alone? What would you do if no one was with you?"

"I'd motor through," he said.

Sally giggled. "Loosen the ginny," he said. "Let out on the ginny. Hurry up."

"I'm doing it as fast as I can," she said. "You should have told me sooner."

They went in to dinner at The Bitter End, tying the dinghy up to the pier with the other boats, walking around the edge of the pen, pretending to admire the fish, feeling tight and conspiratorial.

It was a hot afternoon, hot and still. The fish looked colorless and apathetic. Hardly worth saving, Sally said to herself.

"They look terrible," Jimmy said. "They look all washed out."

"It's the weather," Li said. "And oil from the boats. It gets on their fins."

"That makes me want to throw up," Sally said.

"Well, don't do it now," Li said, looking around to see if anyone was listening. "Come on. Let's go in and order dinner."

They sat at a wicker table in the bar drinking lemonade and pretending to talk about other things, taking turns getting up and wandering around the resort asking questions of everyone they saw.

It was still light in the sky when they finished dinner and started back out to the sailboat.

"I can't wait much longer," Sally said. "I can't stand it."

"Think about them," Jimmy said. "Think about swimming around that pen for a whole year."

"Some of them have been there longer than that," Li said. "The turtles don't even bother to die."

They woke at three and began to stir around the galley. "Let's do it now," Sally said. "There's no reason to wait any longer." She pulled on a bathing suit. She spit into her mask, filled it with tap water and washed it out. She adjusted the snorkel for the fourteenth time. She got out the clippers and cut the edge of a cookie sheet with them. "They work," she said. "They really work."

"I want you to promise to be careful," Li said. "There's no reason to get caught."

"There's nothing to it," Sally said. "I've been diving in caves, Li. Remember that. I went night diving in the caves at Roatan. This is nothing compared to that."

"Nothing is nothing in the ocean," Li said.

"Where's my weight belt?" Sally said. "I had it a minute ago. Oh, damn, what did I do with it?"

"Here it is," Jimmy said. "I was wearing it for you. Why did you put so much on it?"

"It's only three pounds. I need that much to stay down. Well, that's everything then. Are the tanks in the dinghy?"

"Everything's there. I checked everything four times. Quit asking me if everything's there. Come on, let's go."

They walked from the galley to the back of the boat. Jimmy first, Sally behind him and Li Moon bringing up the rear. The moon was huge and white, far to the east in a starry sky. Their shadows lay across the boat, mixed in with the shadows of the lines and rigging.

"What will they think?" Jimmy said. "When they get out?"

"They won't think anything," Sally said. "They'll just start swimming."

Li sat on the hatch cover watching their progress across the water. She touched her sleeves with her fingers, concentrating on the little boat as if she could blow them to shore. *Let her turn the fish loose if she must. Let her believe anything she wishes. It is all a dream. The ten thousand things we desire and dream of. Who am I to tell her that in the morning they will all come swimming back to where they were fed.*

"If you're getting tired," Sally said, "I'll row."

"I'm not tired. Besides, we're almost there. Going back we'll use the motor."

"Be real quiet when we get to the pier. Don't knock against it with the boat."

"You catch it. You're in front."

"You're sure they're only nurse sharks?"

"Well, I asked everybody in the place. Besides, they're so fat they wouldn't eat you in a million years. Look, Sally, do you want me to do it?"

"No, I don't want you to do it. What if they won't swim out?"

"What do you mean?"

"I mean, after we cut it, what if they won't go out?"

"Let them worry about that. Look, you want a cookie? I brought some with me."

"I want a drink," she said. "Hand me that bottle under the seat, will you?"

Aboard the *Wind Chime* Li Moon kept watch. The halyard tapped twice against the mast, then tapped again. Li swore to herself in Chinese and in French. Like all good

sailors she was annoyed by the sound of anything loose on a
boat. She got up and tied it down. When she resumed her
posture the dinghy had made it to the pier.

"Be quiet," Sally said.

"I'm being quiet. You're the one that's talking."

"Here, do this for me." She squirmed around on the seat
and leaned forward so he could strap the tank on. She
tested the gauges and put the mouthpiece into her mouth.
Sally hated diving equipment. It was too heavy, too cum-
bersome, always in the way. She had been a swimmer at the
school she went to in Virginia. Her specialty had been the
butterfly. She moved her arms in a circle, feeling the con-
striction of the straps, remembering that small hot indoor
pool, steam rising, clouding the windows, pulling on her
cap, bending her knees, dying to win.

"Have you got the lights?" she said. "Are you sure they
work?"

"They work."

"Check them again."

He flipped the switches on the underwater lights, holding
them down into the water. Several small fish came swimming up as soon as the light came on.

"They work."

"The minute one of them goes out start blinking the
other one. I might not even know which way is up."

"I know." He attached one of the lights to the weighted
line so he could let it down beside her as she descended.
The other one hung from the back of the dinghy as a
marker.

"I still think you ought to work from the bottom up," he
said.

"Are you kidding? I'm not going to cut the whole thing

anyway. I'm just going down about six feet. If they're too dumb to swim out of that they can just stay in the cage."

"You ready?"

"I think so."

"Then go on. Unless you want me to do it."

"You watch those lights." She held her nose and tumbled backwards into the ocean. In a moment she came up beside him holding the side of the boat.

"I forgot the fucking weight belt. Give it here."

He took it off and handed it to her. "Don't drop it," he said. "Be careful not to drop it."

She adjusted the weight belt, stuck the regulator back in her mouth and reached for the light.

"All right," she said. "Keep hold of that line and don't let it get ahead of me. Pay attention, Jimmy. You watch me like a hawk."

"I'll do it," he said. "I'll do it if you're scared to do it."

She moved down into the water without answering him. She could see fairly well. She studied the post for a moment. The fence was attached to the post in a professional manner, as such things go in the islands. She pulled out the clippers and cut through the first strand, supporting her right hand with her left hand. She could feel the sound as the clippers cut into the metal. The wire snapped apart like a bone.

Several fish swam up to the edge of the pen. Behind them the shapes of the sharks and turtles moved in her imagination. She cut another strand. Then two more. Then three. Something moved beside her in the water. She backed away from the post. It was a turtle swimming by, coming to see about the light.

Oh, shit, she thought. They're going to eat me up. She

moved back to the fence and cut another strand. Well, I can't quit. Jimmy would tell everyone in Guntersville if I did. He'd never be able to keep his mouth shut.

She was breathing heavily now, making a rasping sound against the mouthpiece. Maybe I'll use up all the air. Then I'll have to stop. She clenched her teeth down on the regulator and cut a few more pieces. Well, I have to do it. Goddammit, I am going to do it if it's the last thing I ever do in my life.

She went back to work in earnest, cutting steadily for a few minutes, moving down the post until she was almost four feet underwater. The light moved steadily along beside her. On the other side of the pen the shapes of the fish moved along as she moved. She began to worry that they would be cut on the jagged edges of the wire when they made their escape.

She managed to move down another six inches before the sight of a pair of eyes that seemed an inch wide made her completely lose her nerve. She surfaced, gasping, and pulled herself up on the edge of the boat. Jimmy took hold of her arms.

"What's wrong? What's going on? Are you done?"

"I'm scared to death. That's what's going on. I'm afraid one of them will get cut and they'll start a frenzy."

"They're only nurse sharks."

"I don't care. There's something spooky in there."

"Let me do it. I can do it. I've done it in the pool a million times. Come on. Let me finish doing it."

"Look, Jimmy, reach in that bag and get that gin and pour me some, will you?"

He did as he was told. He handed the cup to her and she drank it like water. "Okay," she said. "Now I'm going to finish it."

"How far down does it go?"

"I can't tell."

"How far are you going to cut it?"

"Not much farther. As far as I think it needs to go." The gin arrived at her brain. *Silver bullets,* she thought. *Who called it that?* She descended again and went back to work. The eyes were still following her but now she didn't care. The fence only went down a few more feet. Below that was cheap wire mesh. *What a makeshift job. Just like a bunch of college boys. Well, I may as well go on and cut it all the way while I'm here.* She took three or four keep breaths of the air. It was so cool, a distillation of air. *A few more feet. Then I can brag about this till the day I die.*

She cut the last strand of wire. Fini, she thought. The section of wire slammed her through the water. Rolled and pushed and shoved her through the water, tore the regulator from her mouth. She breathed in water. Then it was only water. She had always known it would be water.

Jimmy was standing in the dinghy screaming. Aboard the boat Li Moon saw men come running out of the buildings. Lights came on. The body was lifted onto the pier. Li climbed up on the deck beside the mast and stood there in the moonlight, not even weeping, not able to shed a tear. It was completed. It was done.

Belize

THE CAPITAL CITY is like a little town in the Delta, only dirtier; dirtier than anything in the world. The bays that cut into the land from the Atlantic are filthy. Things float on them. Paper cartons, shoes, orange peels. The people barely seem to move. The hotel is unacceptable, but, after all, I tell myself, this isn't Paris, this is an adventure. A diving trip. It is 1964. No one in our crowd has ever been diving. We are going to be the first. Whit has been practicing in the pool. My husband, Davie, knows how from reading a book. Stacy can barely swim. I was a swimmer in high school and I swam in the ocean all my life. What is there to fear? *There is nothing to fear but fear itself, and of course, the Boogie Man.*

We drop the bags in the unacceptable room. We go out to find adventure. There's a grocery store on a corner with

Dutch chocolates. Stacy giggles. Whit buys her a chocolate bar. "Let's take a boat around town," Davie says. "Let's hire one of those men to paddle us around."

"I'd like to eat dinner first," Stacy says. "It's too hot to do a damn thing."

"We aren't going to the island until noon tomorrow," Whit says. "Let's get up early and go out and see the Mayan ruins. I heard there was a wonderful temple."

"Not too early," Stacy says. "It's my vacation."

In the morning a car comes to take us to the forest and the temple. We have eaten breakfast. Whit's been out exploring. "They have two industries," he says. "A man who carves sharks from mahogany and a man and woman team who make herons from the horns of cows."

"What do the rest of them do?" I say. I am sick of Whit. He's so goddamn jolly all the time. So goddamn gung ho. Davie had fucked me that morning while I thought about the orange peels. I feel like I've gained ten pounds. It's hot as the gates of hell.

The temple stands in a clearing. We have come through the forests on a paved road. An Indian is the guide. He is at the station half awake. He is smoking. He doesn't give a damn about us. Stacy accosts him. "I love old Indian stuff," she says. "I studied Mayan art. You had a real civilization down here. It was wonderful."

"You can climb the moon temple," he says. "But be careful. Some stones are loose."

"Well, let's go," Whit says. He starts off in front telling us stuff I don't want to hear about this temple and that temple. Rites in sacred rooms, hearts torn from maidens' breasts. He was reading the literature on the drive. I don't want to know the literature. I want something to happen to

me. Still, it is cool with the jungle all around us. Even Whit
cannot ruin the temple. The stones are so small. The people
must have been the size of children to climb such things.
There is a joke in New Orleans about Frances Tibbets, a
big girl who tried to climb a Mayan ruin and got up and
couldn't get down. She had to be put into a harness and
taken down. It was outside of Mexico City. She panicked
and could not move.

What if that happened to me? I was thinking. I was halfway up and I didn't want to go anymore. I didn't need to
climb this goddamn temple anyway. I could have looked
up at it from the ground. We're going to wear out the
stones of Belize, a bunch of bored rich people from New
Orleans. Some people we know own the whole damn country anyway, they own the fruit company and their cousins
own the mahogany forests. They are nice people. It's not
their fault they're allowed to own Belize. They do good
things with the money. Elect the mayor and help with con-
servation in the Atchafalaya Swamp.

"Well, come on," Davie says. "Hurry up. We have to be
back by noon. Madder's coming to take us to the island."

"Fuck you," I say. I have a large vocabulary for a rich
girl. Besides, I've always had a taste for the lower classes.
When I was small a poor boy down the street used to turn
me on just talking to me across the fence. He knew something my cousins had forgotten. Maybe it just seems that
way. Maybe we are only interested in the unknown. I figured it out once. It goes like this. The brain hunts for something it wants. It sees something. If it can have it, well and
good, then it hunts for something else. Always searching. If
it can't get what it wants, it speeds up a little bit, the libido
works a little harder, the blood pumps, the face gets tight.

On and on, more and more, until it gets what it wants. In Belize the blood is still. Why want anything? it says, you can't get anything, sit still. Where was I? I was saying fuck you to my husband, Davie.

"I'm going down," I say. "I don't want to climb these goddamn little steps anymore."

"You've got to see the top," Whit says. "Come on up. Chicken. Goddammit, Helen, you never finish anything you start." I ignore him. I start down hating the makers of the temple and their goddamn little three-inch steps. I get to the bottom and walk off to explore the half-excavated region between the temple of the moon and the temple of the sun. Clouds have come into the sky. Perhaps it will rain. If you do not build the temple the gods will not send rain. Where did I hear that? My mind is full of things that other people said. I skip from rock to rock, getting away from Whit and Davie and poor old Stacy, who can barely swim. I am a great athlete skipping from rock to rock on my way to bring rain to the temple of the sun. Nyoka, that's who I meant to be. I jump on a loose rock and turn my ankle. Bad, I fall down in a goddamn heap. I can't get up. Fuck and fuck again.

Now is the moment that I put up with Whit for. He was number one in his medical school graduating class. Like so many of us, too smart for his own good. I love him. He is my best friend. Why was I thinking such second-rate shit about my own good friend who is now bending over me and tying up my ankle? Later he gives me a Demerol. I am half asleep on the boat ride to the island, Saint Ginger's Key, an untamed island that Madder Lane has taken as his domain. We are moving out across the water in an open boat with a fifty-horsepower motor. Madder is at the wheel.

Our guide, our leader. We are on our way to the adventure, the birth of a sport. Saint Ginger's Key, toilet paper floating underneath its piers from the outdoor johns, a shower underneath a cistern, a wooden house up on piers with five bedrooms and three doors. Will that keep Whit and Stacy from fucking all night? No. Will that keep the five Tulane students who come to join us from lusting over me in my makeshift cast and nightgown? No. This is an adventure, not a Sunday school picnic. Why do Davie and I have to hate each other so? What did we ever do to deserve this marriage? I raise my hands to his face in the boat. He is a good husband. He is taking care of me. Is it true that after four hundred times you are bored with fucking anyone, even the nicest person you could possibly have married? Whit and Stacy like to fuck each other after doing it for twenty years. Since they were sixteen. They are an exception to every rule, and, besides, their parents are dead. They have to love each other. I am thinking things like that while they carry me up the stairs. Demerol is very nice but it wears off.

Now the diving talk begins. There is Davie and Whit and a black man named Argyle, and Madder. Madder Lane, the famous diving champion of New Orleans and the Gulf Coast. An ex-marine. He is devoting his life to introducing the sport of diving to the South. He shows everyone the generator. The thing that fills the tanks with air. It will purr, purr, purr all night. The sounds of the ocean and the jungle haven't got a chance against the generator. The tanks, our lives depend on the tanks. No, they depend on the regulator, and not running into sharks.

"Well, you ready to go for a trial run?" Madder says. He

flexes his muscles. He has lured us here because Whit operated on his back and he told Whit he could come and bring anyone he wanted for half price if he got well and could walk again. We are the third group of guests Madder has had at Saint Ginger's Key. He hasn't got all the kinks worked out. The groceries are not there, for one thing. You wouldn't believe how much stuff costs. He shows us a jar of peanut butter. Three dollars and eighty-nine cents.

"Let's go," Whit says. "I can't wait to see my first reef."

"No tanks today," Madder says. "First we'll snorkle and get our bearings. You want to go?" He means me.

"No. I have a twisted ankle. I guess I'll be an onlooker for a day or two."

"I'll stay with Helen," Stacy says. She is scared to death of the ocean. Later I will decide she is the only sane person on the island.

"Come on," Whit says. "You promised me." She goes. I will see this many times in my sojourn among the rich. Wives being forced into the ocean, down ski slopes, onto bicycles. Stacy was raised by people that loved her so much they wouldn't let her risk one inch of herself on roller skates. You can't teach people to love the water at thirty-six. She was shaking but she went along. I was younger and more evil then. I thought she was a coward.

Madder plays a mouth organ at night. There are kerosene lamps on the tables. The Tulane students have joined us. The groceries have come. "You guys lend a hand, tomorrow we'll get this place finished. Got to make some doors. Who's going to help?"

"You going to give us a rebate on our money?"

"Hell no. I'm taking you diving on the best goddamn

unspoiled reef in the fucking world. You've never seen
angels the size of the ones down there. Blow your fucking
mind."

"How about sharks?"

"A few nurses, nothing bad. No hammerheads. Never
saw one down here. Don't know what keeps them away.
Fucking smell of Belize. No, didn't mean that. I love these
goddamn people. I'm never going home." I was getting in a
better mood. We were drinking gin. Gin's the best, the epit-
ome. If you can drink gin and hold it, you're in business. I
can hold it occasionally. I was mixing it with Demerol.
Whit was being a doll about everything. I started liking
Davie. He was the only one at the table that wasn't brag-
ging about anything. He is a brilliant man. I was remembering that, there in that dark room with those kerosene
lamps and everyone around the table waiting for the adventure in the morning. He is a brave man. I was going to
fuck him without thinking about a thing but how much I
liked him and how smart he was. I moved closer to him and
held his hand. He couldn't believe his luck. His wife had
stopped being a bitch for a moment. I guess it scared him.
He had another drink. The talk wore on. Fish Madder had
seen, reefs he had been on, accidents he had averted, divers
on the rigs, navy divers, his buddy that dove on enemy sub-
marines in the war when they had to invent the equipment,
regulators, which kind was the best.

Whit's turn, sailboat races he had won, tight spots he'd
been in, stuff he knew, medical terms, how much he liked to
fuck his wife, how sexy she was in bed, she giggled, how
much better looking she was naked than any woman in the
world. "Whit," she said. "That's about enough."

The Tulane students were impressed whether they

wanted to be or not. Now we were talking books. We were reading anthropology that year. We could tell you anything about culture and its sources. "Whit," Stacy repeated. "I wish you wouldn't drink any more. I'm going to bed."

"Me too," I said. "Can I have a Demerol?"

Now it is morning and time for the dive. We eat a hearty breakfast of fish and peanut butter and stale bread and jelly and pineapple. Divers' breakfast. Load up, the water's cold. Thank God for my ankle. Thank God I don't have to get in that goddamn little scary boat and go out into those waves. It is dark on the ocean even though this is morning. "How was it?" I asked Stacy when they returned for lunch. "What was the reef like?"

"It's very beautiful." She lowered her eyes.

"Tell the truth."

"I loved seeing it. Whit bought me this little waterproof card with the names of all the fish on it so I can identify them."

"Was it cold?"

"It's pretty cold."

"I'll go as soon as my ankle's better."

"It's really interesting. You shouldn't miss it since you're here."

"I'll go as soon as I can."

"Your ankle won't bother you in the water. You won't need it there." Stacy had never talked to me that way before but I figured it was caused by the island. We were on the wooden stairs. I was in my nightgown and an open robe. Very pretty, blue and white dotted swiss, very light. It had cost three hundred dollars at the Lylian Shop. That's how rich we used to be. Some ladies in Holland had sewn the thing together. They like to sew it. I like to wear it, that's how I used to try to feel.

So we are standing at the top of the stairs and down below Madder is moving the tanks. His back is fine. He's not worried about his back. If it goes out again old Doc Whit will fix him up. He can be repaired and repaired and always mend.

"Hey, Madder," one of the students called out. "Are we all going back out in one boat?"

"Relax," Madder said. "Argyle's going to take half of you in the whaler. Split up. Stacy, you stay with me. I'm going to take you down myself. Whit can team up with Davie." They left in a wake of churning saltwater, all waving back to me. I sat down on the stairs. Shit, I didn't have a goddamn thing to do. I hobbled into the kitchen and watched the cook and ate some peanut butter and went into my room and stared at the vacant door.

They returned at five, full of diving stories and the names of fish. Full of adventure, crazy about each other, welded into a team. Ready for more and more and more.

On the third day I went along. How many days since we had left our happy homes. Saturday, Sunday, Monday, Tuesday, Wednesday. Now it was Thursday and they put me in the boat and strapped the tank on my back and told me not to be afraid and I was afraid. I was scared to death. Later, I went down to a hundred feet and got narced and wanted to go deeper and deeper and deeper and Madder got furious and dragged me back up to the boat.

At dinner they started talking about going out at night. We sat around the table and drank brandy and Madder told about how the fish make cocoons to sleep in and how you can touch them with your finger and how the sea anemones open up and all the darkest secrets of the ocean make themselves known. "You start with four lights. One on each end of the boat. And a keeper in the boat. He doesn't drink and he doesn't dive. There must be two people with lights in the water. If one light goes out, all right. The man who lost his goes back to the boat and takes one off the stern. But if two lights go out, you go back. You never swim with only two lights. That's the iron rule."

"I want to go," Whit said. "Will you take us?"

"Not for all the money in the world. You aren't even certified."

"A hundred apiece?"

"Not for anything. Besides, I haven't got the lights. I broke one last week and I haven't replaced it."

"I'll go to shore and buy some."

"No."

"I'll fix the ones you have."

"Absolutely not."

"How about you, Davie? You want in?"

"He won't take us."

"He's right. I won't."

Of course he would. For a hundred dollars apiece and Whit repairing the light and Stacy being the one to stay in the boat. Not me. I wasn't that crazy. I just kept wishing I had seen Davie's will. "Am I in the will?" I said.

"Of course you're in the will. Am I in yours?"

"I don't have one. I don't believe in them."

The Tulane students were out. They couldn't afford it and besides there weren't enough lights.

"I want to do it Saturday night before we leave on Sunday," Whit said. "I can remember it flying home. Shit, it's great. I just can't wait. How do we buddy it, with three?"

"You and I will have the lights and leave Davie with the knife and a shark stick."

"What for?"

"They range at night."

"I thought you'd never seen anything here but nurses."

"Just in case. The ocean's got to be respected."

There are pictures of us that week. Me, standing in the doorway looking sexy in my temporary cast and my wide straw hat and the bottom of a bikini. My stomach sticking out. Stacy in the long pants and long-sleeved shirt she wore to dive in. As though being fully dressed would protect her from the water. The Tulane students gathered around the generator. Argyle holding up a fish. The reefs, indescribable, impossible to photograph, although everyone with a camera was beginning to try. The quiet world, the quick, silent world of absolute fear. Everything in the water is afraid except perhaps the porpoises and the whales. The rest are always eating each other up or breeding hysterically or waiting to be eaten. Swish, and they are gone. Now Madder and Whit and Davie are going down to surprise these creatures at their rest. They are going down at night. If you lose your way in the water and the lights go out you don't know if you are going up or down and down feels better. That's what narced means. Nitrogen narcosis. What happened to me. Three martinis, the heat of love, orgasms in the brain, pleasure such as no drug can give you. Instantaneous pleasure. One second you are yourself. The next second you are narced and you will swim down forever and die or give your regulator away to a fish you are so happy to

be happy. If two lights go out they are coming in. That's
that. Everyone agrees and shakes hands on it and Madder
brings some papers around for everyone to sign.

"What's this?"

"Oh, just something that says I'm not responsible if you
die." Davie takes his and reads it and signs it and hands it
over. Stacy takes Whit's.

"I don't like this. I don't want you to go if it's this dangerous."

"Oh, for Christ's sake, Stacy, hand that here."

"What if you die?"

"I won't die."

"Helen doesn't care if I die. As long as she's in the will."

"That's a lie. I don't give a fuck if you go or not. It's up
to you if you're that crazy. How dangerous is it, Madder?"

"I told you I didn't want to do it. We don't have to go.
It's choppy out there anyway. Might be a lot of sand on the
reef. Might not even be pretty."

"Don't back out," Whit said. "You promised."

"Sign the paper, Whit," Davie said. "And let's get the
stuff together and go on out there." See, I told you Davie
was the bravest one even if he doesn't talk as much. I
started loving him again and wanted to fuck him. I moved
close to him and put my arm around his waist. "I am too
worried about you," I said. "Only I suppose you know what
you're doing. Don't get narced."

"If two lights go out we're coming back."

"I wired those things together so tight you'll never get
them loose to change the batteries. They'll work." Whit was
happy now. Stacy was miserable and scared to death and
going to stand by her man anyhow. Tell me there's no fun
in being rich. Life is what you make it. You can create ex-

citement anywhere. We walked down to the pier, talking
masks and regulators and weight belts and lights. Talking,
nothing to fear, nothing to fear, nothing to fear.

They took off across the water, moving slowly, being re-
spectful of the Atlantic Ocean which reaches from shore to
shore full of danger and beauty and mystery. And so forth.
I went back inside. The Tulane students were playing
poker. I put a hundred-dollar bill on the table and asked if
I could sit in.

They are playing five-card draw. A tough game. Two
rugby players and a distance runner and a boy cheerleader.
They're drinking Mexican beer. It's the rugby player that I
like. A man of few words. I don't even know how to play
this game so I start winning. I'm ahead about eighty dollars. It embarrasses me. I start trying to lose. I get back to
even. Then I get a full house and take it all back and more.
The rugby player is starting to hate my guts. "What time is
it?" I say.
    "You aren't going to quit?"
    "Of course not. I just wondered how long they'd been out
there."
    "How long did they say they'd be?"
    "They didn't say."
    "It's been an hour and a half since they left."
    "How long does it take to reach the reef?"
    "Twenty minutes. Fifteen."
    I lose back all the money and some of my own and get up
and go to stand in the door. Staring out to sea. The sailor's
wife on the widow's walk. "This is too long. I want one of
you to go look for them."

"In what? There isn't anything but the raft. Argyle took the whaler home."

"It's got a motor on it."

"Okay. In a few minutes. If they don't come back by eleven. Don't worry about them, Mrs. Altmont. It's okay. Madder knows what he's doing. He's the best. He dove the Great Barrier Reef. They're probably having fun."

They were not having fun. The first light went out as soon as they put the anchor down. Whit worked on it but it wouldn't come back on. Then Stacy cried and begged to go back and got hysterical so Whit had to stay with her in the boat. They were down to three lights. One hanging off the bow and one each for Davie and Madder to carry. The water was choppy. There was sand in the water, drifting all over the reef. They couldn't see and Madder felt sorry for Davie, spending a hundred bucks to watch Stacy have a fit, so he took him around the corner of the reef to a place he hoped would be protected from the sand. Then Davie's light went out. They climbed up on the coral, which is as sharp as razor blades and brittle, to yell at Whit and Stacy, blood running down their legs, shark bait, shark lures. Davie could barely make out the boat in the waves without a light and Whit had the motor running because Stacy didn't trust the anchor so he couldn't hear them yelling and a storm was blowing up. It was as dumb as anything could be and as poorly planned and just like something Davie would get into. Thank God I wasn't out there. I have that much to be grateful for.

"Over here," Davie kept yelling, but Whit was running the motor and telling Stacy all about how there isn't any security anyway so you might as well take chances. "Let's

swim for it," Madder said and Davie said, okay. They took
the remaining light and went down below the waves and
swam to the boat using Madder's navy diving compass
watch which he never takes off when he's on the island.
They swam northeast. Madder told me that about a hundred times. "Northeast. We swam northeast."

By then the Tulane students had gone out in the rubber
boat with the ten-horsepower motor. They were halfway to
the reef when the dive boat came slowly chugging across
the waves and met them. They tied the raft onto the boat
and came on in. Argyle and I were waiting on the pier. I
had given Davie up. I had already given his bike away and
started selling the house. I could not live there after that.
He was the first one on the pier, so excited by almost dying
he felt like he had a fever. We all went into the house and
started drinking. We drank up all the brandy and all the
rum and all the gin. We drank up all the beer. We played
Madder's collection of Frank Sinatra albums. "I've Got a
Crush on You, Sweetie Pie," and "Nancy, with the Laughing Face," and some Dean Martin hits. Around two that
morning Davie and I cuddled up in our bed with our arms
around each other. My hero. "Did you think you were
going to die?" I said. "Did you? Well, did you or not?"

"I don't want to talk about it, Helen."

"What do you want to talk about then? Tell me that.
What is there for you and I to talk about?"

"I'll tell you about it later."

"You won't even tell me if you were going to die?"

"No."

"Then I'm sleeping on the porch." I disentangled myself
and took the heavy cover and my pillow and went outside
and looked at the stars. It was a long way from here to
there. I tried one of the hammocks but that wasn't any

good so I walked on down the stairs and lay down on the beach. I was good and drunk and I was sick of this goddamn diving adventure. It reminded me of the first time I went to the beach and my mother was the chaperone and everyone got sand fleas and my brother's best friend tried to rape me. Yes, we are a long way from the stars. So near and yet so far. I rolled up in the blanklet to listen to the sea. If I counted up to sixty a hundred thousand times it would be Sunday night and I would be back in a hotel in a city having a shower and something to eat besides peanut butter and fish.

IV
The Dishes Can Wait

Traceleen at Dawn

A LOT OF PEOPLE have asked me to tell the story of how
Miss Crystal stopped drinking. It seems a number of other
ones think it would be a good idea for them too. Miss Crystal is the lady I work for. I take care of the house and nurse
Crystal Anne. I have nursed her since she was born and I
have been with Miss Crystal ever since she married Mr.
Manny and moved to New Orleans from Jackson, Mississippi, where her family is. She has a son from her former
marriage and that has complicated things.

So we have all been here in the house on Story Street for
six years. It seems longer. It seems like so many things could
not have happened in so short a time. I have noticed time
seems to pass in different ways at different times. Eighteen
years since I graduated down at Boutte and that seems like

a million years. Two years since Miss Crystal quit drinking and that seems like yesterday.

The reason she had to quit to begin with is that she is able to drink all night if she wants to. Every member of her family is the same way, especially the men. The men of Miss Crystal's family are not like men in New Orleans. They are more like men from a while ago.

Well, to begin with, Miss Crystal's decision not to take a drink was not some sudden decision, like you see on television or like that. No, it was a long time coming. Several incidents led up to it. First, her closest friend told her she thought it was time for her to stop. They were out running on the Tulane track. It was Miss Sister Laughlin that said it. She is Miss Crystal's oldest friend except for Miss Lydia who is out in California living on vegetables. She has become quite thin. Miss Sister stopped Miss Crystal dead on the track and told her she had been drinking too much and it was not good for Crystal Anne to have a mother that was that way. Miss Sister couldn't have said it at a better time. It was only a few weeks after the incident in the French Quarter when Miss Crystal and Mr. Deveraux were locked in the bordello trying to stop the child abuse ring. Mr. Manny had had to come and get them out and was so mad about it he had moved to Mandeville for good. That story was all over town so I guess Miss Sister had heard it.

Miss Crystal came home from the track very low. She stayed inside all day without combing her hair. Finally she decided she must quit taking a drink if it was the last thing she would ever do. "How can I do it, Traceleen?" she said. "I cannot join the AA. They are not my type of people."

"They might turn out to be nice," I said. "Judge Wiggins, that I used to work for, joined them. He is a very nice man."

"No, I went there once," she said. "They are so sad and try to cover it up with jokes and drink this goddamn coffee all the time instead of whiskey. No, I will do it cold turkey. I will do it on my own."

"Call Miss Sister and get her to come over and help you," I said. "She's the one that brought it up." So Miss Sister comes over and they sit in the kitchen drinking coffee and are real serious and Miss Sister calls her brother that is a psychiatrist. We were acquainted with him already. We took Crystal Anne to him once when she was acting crazy and would not wear shoes. I thought he was a very nice man and sensible. He said to let her keep them off until she stumped her toe and so we did.

So Miss Sister calls her brother and the upshot of it is he makes Miss Crystal an appointment and she puts on this light green dress with white flowers on it and goes over to find out how to quit. When she comes back she has this tape. She is supposed to lie down on the den floor with a pillow under her head and listen to it each morning and each night and it will put messages in her brain. Alcohol is your enemy. It is bad for your body and bad for your mind. Alcohol will kill you. Like that.

So Miss Crystal comes home and throws all the whiskey in the house down the sink, even Mr. Manny's wine that he orders from France, and then she goes in the den and lies down on the floor and listens to her tape.

Then about ten days go by. It is raining a lot and that didn't help. Miss Crystal, she don't let it get her down however and starts cleaning up the house, cleaning out all the closets and the basement and the attic and Crystal Anne's room. I was standing by all I could and even made an excuse to come in on Sunday so as to help her get through the weekend.

Saturday goes by and it is a long day. Miss Crystal, she is used to getting dressed up on Saturday afternoon and having people over. Now what is she supposed to do? The sun was shining. It might have been better if it had not been. By five o'clock she was pacing the floors. "Go to the park," I advised her. "Take Crystal Anne and push her on the swings. I will be here making you a caramel cake. When you get back there will be a cake with icing an inch thick." That cheered her up. I have never seen Miss Crystal turn down sugar. So she went out to the park and played with her daughter and came home and ate the cake and we made it until Sunday. I let myself in on Sunday morning about nine o'clock. I'd been up since dawn wondering what I'd find when I got there.

She was sitting in her robe reading a book, happy as she could be not to have a hangover. "What are you reading?" I said. "A story about a Kool-Aid wino," she said. She was laughing. "This crazy man out in California wrote it. It's about a little boy who is hooked on grape Kool-Aid. It could be me."

Then Sunday went by and I thought we were out of the woods when who should show up but Mr. Manny. He comes by pretending to need some shirts but as soon as he has a stack of them in his arms he turns around and demands to know why Miss Crystal has let Crystal Anne quit school. She is dressed by then, in some plaid wool walking shorts and one of his open-neck casual shirts. He have so few things. It never fails to make him mad when Miss

Crystal and King just borrow anything they like of his without even asking. "Is that my shirt?" he says. Then, "I can't believe you let Crystal Anne quit school. Children can't just quit school."

"She is only three years old," Miss Crystal says. "Three-year-old children do not need to go to school."

"She'll never get in Newman if you let her get behind. She has to go somewhere, Crystal. I don't care where it is but she has to start back tomorrow. Tomorrow, do you understand?"

"She said a fat girl was trying to drown her. I don't know if I'll even get her to put her head under in the tub again. She'll probably never learn to swim."

"You are crazy, Crystal. Do you know that? And my daughter is going back to school. She can't sit in that tent all her life. There's a big world out there and my child is going to be prepared to meet it." They are facing each other in the hall now. Just like old times. Crystal Anne, she is eating it up, standing in the doorway of the den where she's been watching TV in her tent. I am tired of that tent myself to tell the truth. Can't even get in the den to vacuum.

So Mr. Manny has come over and started this ruckus and they fight it out for about fifteen minutes, calling each other Lawyer and Whore and White Liberal Bullshit and Crazy and Mother's Boy and Drunkard and Alcoholic and like that. Then Mr. Manny, he go get Crystal Anne and hug her and tell her not to worry he is going to get a court order and take her across the lake where she can live a normal life and go to school. As soon as he is out the door Miss Crystal she walk across the kitchen and call the airport and

order a private plane. Then she pour herself a drink. I don't
say a word. It is not me she has to answer to. Besides, it does
not do the slightest bit of good to tell someone not to drink
if they have set their mind to it. Pray is the best thing to do
under those circumstances. Hide the car keys and pray.

Anyway, then she pack a bag for herself and Crystal
Anne and say she is going to do what she should have done
weeks ago, go up to Vail, Colorado and get King. He is
working in a ski village up there since he left school. This
has not been an easy house to work for. We have shed our
tears. I've told you that before.

So Miss Crystal pack their bags and dress Crystal Anne
in a new white velvet dress and off they go. No sooner are
they out the door than Mr. Manny call up and want to talk
to her. He seem more reasonable than when he left, talking
very sweet and polite.

"Traceleen, go find my wife and tell her I'm on the
phone and would she pick up the receiver and talk to me."
Like that, controlled I guess you'd call it.

"They're gone," I said. She had not told me not to tell.
"She has got a plane to take her to see King. She has had a
drink, Mr. Manny. I guess I should tell you that. To tell the
truth she has had several." I felt bad about taking sides like
that, nobody in the world could love anybody more than I
love Miss Crystal but there comes a time when you must do
what's right even if it could be misunderstood. "Thank
you," Mr. Manny said. We hung up and I sat down at the
table and put my head in my hands. I was trying to pray
but no prayers came. It is too confusing to be alive sometimes, sometimes there are things that make me wish we
were all back in Boutte sitting on my auntee's porch without a car. Why couldn't Mr. Manny and Miss Crystal just
fall in love again and spruce up the bedroom and have Miss

Sister over making bread and playing practical jokes on
their cousins like they used to do when we were first setting
up housekeeping? What has gone wrong around here that
no one can love anyone anymore?

Then Mr. Manny is there and begging me to go with him
and we get in his car and go out to the private airport. We
got there just as they were taking off. A Queenaire, that's
what she hired to take them to Colorado. Mr. Manny, he
hired us a smaller plane, with just one engine, and the two
of us got into it behind the pilot and we are chasing them
through the skies. Our pilot has got Miss Crystal's pilot on
the radio, trying to make him turn back on the grounds
that Miss Crystal is drinking and unfit to charter an airplane. Miss Crystal's pilot, he won't do it, he says only the
pilot must be sober. About that time I have remembered
how to pray. I do not like the looks of the sky around us,
there is lightning going off in all directions. I had never
known what lightning looked like before that day. From
down below you only see a very small part of what is going
on in the clouds. I would have to draw it to describe it to
you. I know airplanes with only one motor should not be up
in that kind of weather. "Turn around," I said. "We have
got no business flying into that lightning." About that time
a big bolt of it went off out the window, a whole network of
lightning streaks like a spiderweb or the veins on old people's hands. I thought I would throw up or start to scream.
Mr. Manny he put his hand on my knee and squeeze it.
Then he talks on the radio some more, then he confers with
the pilot and we begin to turn around. Miss Crystal's voice
is on the radio again and I hear Mr. Manny promise her
that if she will turn around too and come back home he
will go get King himself and anything else she wants him to

do, even quit his job. The radio is crackling and crackling.
These big lightning clouds are almost touching the wings of
the plane. It is the most terrible time I have ever had with
the Weisses and even beats the day Miss Crystal threw the
television set out the window during the Vietnam war. It is
so terrible and the sky is so full of every kind of thing and so
many colors I could not describe what they looked like,
there is no paint or name for them.

Then I see the Queenaire turning around beside us and
we fly back to the New Orleans airport. I thought I must
have been gone a year. Mark had a fit when I got home and
told him what had happened. He told me never to let him
know the details unless I wanted somebody killed.

Part two. Now it is the next morning and Miss Crystal is
more determined than ever to quit drinking. It has cost her
twelve hundred dollars for that airplane ride. It is getting
too expensive to drink and besides, King will be coming
home and she will need her wits about her if we are to get
him back into a school and off of dope and everything. I
wish Miss Crystal had some God she could hold onto in
times like these. But no, she prefers to go it alone. So we got
Crystal Anne fixed up with Adelaide Simmons to play with
and Miss Crystal gets dressed and goes back to the drinking
doctor. She is gone half the day. It turned out she was having to have blood tests made.

So this time she come home with these white pills that do
something to your blood. If you drink when you have them
inside your bloodstream you will become violently ill and
think you are going to die. It is called the aversion theory of
stopping drinking. Miss Crystal, she thinks it is perfectly
suited to her personality as it lets you decide ahead of time

whether you are going to drink and not at a party when you are not as likely to hate yourself for doing it.

I wish they could get something like that for the ones that like to eat. Anyway, we have got to wait three days for her to take a pill. You must wait until the slightest trace of alcohol has gone from your blood. So three days go by and meanwhile we are moving furniture. Mr. Manny has decided to move back in. They have made a truce. He is only moving into the guest room though. Not into the bedroom. He said they have had so many fights in there, including the time King tore the bedpost off the bed, that he is never sleeping there again. Besides, I think he suspects Miss Crystal has been sleeping there with Mr. Alan while he was across the lake. Of course, he is the one that left so he can't throw stones.

So we are moving a king-size bed into the guest room and Mr. Manny's big mahogany wardrobe that he takes everywhere he go. He has moved it five times since I have worked for the Weisses, once to Mandeville and once to an apartment on Exposition Boulevard and once down to the Pontalba for the summer. Every time there is a flare-up in this relationship I end up with my back out from moving furniture. I have learned my lesson by now though and have Mark's cousin, Singleton, over to do the heavy work.

So everything is going along fine for several weeks. Miss Crystal, she takes her big white pills and is writing an article for the *Times-Picayune* about how to stop drinking. She had been a reporter when she was young. I think I have told you that. Crystal Anne is in school every morning at Saint James where they do not have a pool. King is home and has a job working for a man that makes Mardi Gras floats. It is in this warehouse down on Tchoupitoulas and Miss Crystal goes down every day and takes him his lunch. It is beginning to seem like an army camp around our house, everybody on time and doing what they should.

There is this one float King was especially interested in that has the king of the sea surrounded by mermaids and oysters and shrimp and holding a shrimp boat in his hand. He drew it for me on a tablet, then made me come down on my way home from work and take a look in person. He looked smaller than sixteen, in that big old warehouse with them grown men he works with. I do not understand that boy although I love him and could look at him all day, he is so beautiful and golden. Poor Miss Crystal. She has been in for it since the day she had him when she was only eighteen. That's too young to be a mother for someone as highstrung as she is.

Anyway, she is taking her white pills and the children are coming along and Mr. Manny, he is just like always. He gets up early and puts on his brown suit and goes downtown to make the money. He is trying to be cheerful but I know he is just waiting for the other shoe to drop. Also, I wish Miss Crystal would break down and go sleep in the guest room. I think it is her place to give in on that and I was on the point of telling her so. Miss Crystal and Mr. Manny love each other. If they did not have a strong love they could never have overcome their families and made a mixed marriage. Still, love dies. We must admit that. The problem with Miss Crystal and Mr. Manny is they are too smart for each other and love excitement and love to argue. Sometimes I think it is best if very smart people do not marry each other. There is not enough room in one marriage for so many opinions.

So the winter is going by at our house and it looks like Miss Crystal is going to make her thirty-fifth birthday and maybe even Mardi Gras without a drink. That is her goal. At that time she could tell you to the day how long it had been since she took a drink. She talked about it quite a bit, muttering to herself. Also, she had been finding out about those pills. Antabuse, that is what they are called. It seems that what they do is more complicated than we thought at first. Miss Crystal found this article in a medical magazine that says they might change the middle of your brain where the messages go through from one side to the other and keep the left working with the right. Miss Crystal is very particular about her brain. She was an exceptional student when she was in school and studied philosophy and the Greek language.

Anyway, back to those pills. Miss Crystal had become very worried over this article she read. Also there was an incident at a party she went to. Someone served her a dessert with sherry in it and she became very red in the face and had to leave the table. She was quite frightened by that and had been half afraid to swallow one since. She had been doing so well with not drinking and gotten all the way through Christmas and was enjoying not having any hangovers so she decided to throw the pills away and go back to the tape. Here is how complicated the pills became. We couldn't decide how to throw them away. If we flushed them down the toilet they might get back into the water supply and kill someone down the line. Anything can happen with chemicals. It seems to me that people should be

very careful about making anything they cannot get rid of.
Finally, we just crushed them up and put them in the attic
marked poison, in a sealed can up high where no child
could find them. I suppose they are still up there. I should
check and see.

Part three. We had come down to the weekend of February 10. Miss Crystal is almost finished with her article for
the newspaper and about to turn it in. She was worried
about whether they would print it or not as she had not
written anything for a long time and she thought she might
have lost her touch. I thought it was very good, the part she
let me read, but with too many big words. I like writing to
stay simple myself, be more like talking so the reader
doesn't get the idea they are being preached at. Anyway,
Miss Crystal is on a diet on top of quitting drinking and she
is nervous and can't sit still. She keep going out to the park
and running around the lagoon. Every time she go out
there she keeps running into this girl that has this disease
that makes her think she is fat even though she is thin as a
rail. She is married to this lawyer Miss Crystal knows and
she has this six-month-old baby boy she pushes around the
park all day while she runs. She is driving everyone that
sees her crazy. Miss Crystal wants to get some exercise but
every time she goes to the park there is this crazy girl push-
ing this baby and it makes her ask herself, Am I Crazy Too?
Why would someone stop doing everything they like?
Maybe I am as crazy as that girl, here I am, almost thirty-
five years old and married to a rich man and I cannot even
have a drink or a tuna fish sandwich. That is the type thing
she would ask herself when she came home from exercising
in the park. She had me doing it, wondering what I was
giving up, not letting myself do. I am still thinking about

that. Who is it telling that girl she is fat? Why is she listening to what she hears?

So Miss Crystal is on this diet and she is depressed from being hungry and not being able to decide whether being on a diet is a good idea or something other people have put in her head. She is torn down the middle on that issue. Finally, she comes in the kitchen, it is two o'clock in the afternoon on February 10, I'll remember that day, and she starts making a lemon meringue pie, which is King's favorite. The next thing I know she has me getting out the freezer and Crystal Anne is sitting in the middle of the kitchen floor turning the crank on homemade chocolate ice cream and I am beating up a pound cake. Butter and eggs and sugar and flour and vanilla flavoring and on Miss Crystal's counter there is lemon and evaporated milk and lemon rind and crushed-up graham crackers. I don't know what all. It was spring in that kitchen. I felt like we had gotten somewhere, made some sort of opening. Begun to see the light. That sort of sentiment was in my head.

Life is not that simple. God has made it harder than that. Sometimes I get very mad at Him and think He is not a good judge of things.

Just about the time we are getting the kitchen straightened up and powdered sugar sprinkled on the cake Miss Crystal turns on the radio and this song comes on. A song she used to listen to with Mr. Alan last year when they were having their love affair. She stand very still, her meringue knife in her hand. "Oh, you came here with my best friend, Jim, and here I am, trying to steal you away from him. Oh, if I don't do it, you know somebody else will, if I don't do it, you know somebody else will."

It is a funny song to have for a love song. I remember Mr.

Alan standing in this very kitchen dancing and singing along to it, making shrimp Creole and being in love with her. That was when she split up with Mr. Manny the first time.

Miss Crystal listened to the whole song without saying a word. Then she reach up in a cabinet and take down a bottle of whiskey and pour herself a drink. "I am going to die when all this is over," she said. "And I have not had my share of the stuff I wanted. I am tired of being hungry. To hell with it. I'm starving to death for everything I need." She drank the glass of whiskey and poured herself another one. I did not say a word. I looked at the clock. It was four-thirty. What would the evening bring?

Part four. What happened next I had to piece together from reports. As soon as we cleaned up the kitchen I left. I was not staying around. I put on my things and went on home. "Stop worrying about that woman," Mark said to me. "She can take care of herself." But how was I to stop? If you are with someone you begin to love them, you hear their joys and sorrows, you share your heart. That is what it means to be a human being. There is no escaping this. Ever since the first day I went to work for her I have loved Miss Crystal as if she was my sister or my child. I have spread out my love around her like a net and I catch whatever I have to catch. That is my decision and the job I have picked out for myself and if Wentriss wants to call me a slave that is because she does not know what she is talking about. Miss Crystal always pays me back. She would go to battle for me. We know these things. We are not as dumb as we seem.

*   *   *

Anyway, back to the night of February 10. I was put out with her that night. She was going to ruin all our good work and there was nothing anyone could do to stop her. The Lord's will be done, I suppose I was saying something like that. That is the will of the Lord. I still think I was right to go on home. Of course, if it had turned out differently I would be feeling like it was my fault. That is also how we are, something we cannot change or do anything about.

The night of February 10. Miss Crystal kept on drinking and cooking and called up a number of her friends and ordered champagne. Mr. Manny was in Chicago for the night. Then everyone came over and ate and drank and talked but it did not last too long. Miss Crystal's heart wasn't in it and besides it had been so long since she had a drink she couldn't hold up like she used to. King had come home and grabbed his chance and gone off to play the machines at The Mushroom Cloud. Miss Crystal sent her friends home about nine and fell out on the sofa, just passed right out leaving Crystal Anne alone.

Crystal Anne was being real quiet, taking things in and out of her tent. Dishes of ice cream we found later and half the cake and a champagne bottle. All her dolls and her spacemen and Luke Skywalker and Pilot Barbie. I was the one that cleaned up the tent, what was left of the tent.

It had turned off chilly when the sun went down. None of the ones at the party had turned the heat on and Miss Crystal was asleep so Crystal Anne decided to build herself a campfire. She knew just how to do it. She had watched King do it at the beach. She carried some newspapers out of the kitchen and arranged them on the den rug right in

front of her tent. Between the tent and the TV. Then she
got some blocks and tinker-toys and put them on. Then she
went into the living room and got some of Mr. Manny's fat
pine kindling he orders from Maine and she arrange it just
so. Then she go get all her stuffed dolls and toys and set
them up around the edge in a circle and then she took a cigarette lighter she found somewhere and set it on fire. The
fire was between where she must have been and the door to
the sun room. She was trying to jump from the sofa arm
through the door when Miss Crystal woke up and heard her
screaming. "Stay there," Miss Crystal says she remember
yelling it over and over. "Go in the bathroom. Go in the
bathroom, Crystal Anne. If you don't go in the bathroom I
will kill you." Miss Crystal bust on through the fire and
grab her up and run into the bathroom with her and out
the back door onto the porch and there is no way down that
way but the hanging ladder King got in New York at a
fancy toy store. It has been there for years. Miss Crystal
didn't know whether to risk it or just throw Crystal Anne
off the balcony or try to make it down the hall. From the
bedroom door it did not look like the hall was burning yet.
She made the best decision that she could. She put Crystal
Anne on her back and climbed down with that baby hanging onto her, clawing her face and pulling at her hair but
hanging on like a little monkey, as Miss Crystal always described it later. "Arboreal we were, arboreal we are." That's
how she puts it. It means we used to live in trees if you go
along with that theory.

So finally they have made it to the ground on that rope
ladder that's been hanging there five years in the sun and
rain and then Miss Crystal breaks into a downstairs window to see if King is in his room but he is not there. Then,
finally, she calls the fire department and they come and

ruin all the upholstery and drapes in the upstairs not to mention the carpets. We were living in the Pontchartrain Hotel for several months after that. It was quite a mess.

That was the end of Miss Crystal's drinking. I wish the story could be of more use to other people. It seems it takes something like a fire or falling down a flight of stairs or getting torn up in a drunk driving accident to separate people from their desire to have a drink with one another.

Of the things Miss Crystal tried the one I would recommend the most is that tape she had. It had some very nice things on it beside the ones dealing with alcohol. Your Body Is Your Temple, that is the one I liked. Whatever you put into it, the next day that is what you will be made out of. What would you rather look like in the end, a bottle of whiskey or a stalk of celery or a dish of chocolate ice cream? That's the question I'm asking myself right now. As soon as I finish ironing this shirt I am going to make today's choice. Today it will be one thing. Tomorrow it might be something else.

Anna, Part I

IT WAS A COLD DAY in the Carolinas, drizzling rain that seemed to hang in the sky, that barely seemed to fall. The trees were bare, the mountains hazy in the blue distance, the landscape opened up all the way to Virginia. It was a big day for Anna Hand. It was the day she decided to give up being a fool and go back to being a writer. She called her editor.

"I want a contract. I can't stand it anymore. I'm going back to work."

"For a novel or a book of stories?"

"Stories. Stories will do."

"Are you all right?"

"Can I have the contract or not?"

"You are spoiled rotten. Do you know that?"

"I want it today."

"You've got it."

"Good. I'm hanging up."

"Wait a minute. Are you all right?"

"I will be. I've wasted ten months of my life. Ten god-damn months in the jaws of love. Well, I had to do it. It's like a cold. If you leave the house sooner or later it happens. Anyway, I'm through. Call David and get something in writing for me, will you? I'm hanging up."

"Call me if you need me. Anna, listen to me a minute. If you need me, call me."

"For ten months every meaningful or true thing in my life was a secret. Can you believe that? The main part of my life was secret and the junk was public. Imagine living like that Try to imagine it, Arthur. Imagine living that way."

"Was it my fault? Did I do it?"

"You contributed. You were there. Well, I'll have you something by September. Something really good."

"What's it going to be called?"

" 'Light can be both wave and particle.' To make them think. If they can't think they can't be my readers."

"Don't get cynical."

"I am already. I'm cultivating it." She hung up the phone and went upstairs and into her small old-fashioned kitchen. The cupboards were bare. There was nothing on the shelves but some protein powder and crackers and sev-eral kinds of tea and four different brands of instant coffee. She put some water on to boil, thinking of her father. It's a wonder I could love anyone at all, even for ten months, she decided. Even a married man who was doomed to break my heart. Even a redhaired married baby doctor who looks like my twin brother.

She stared out the window at the hills, thinking of the

places she had been. She had been in Stockholm and London and Zurich and Rome. In Boston and Seattle and New York City. Now she was home. Now she would find the pieces of herself, take herself back from the world. But I do not exist without the world, she thought. All of them are part of me. Quanta exist in the set of all existing quanta. They go in and out of existence as part of the whole. Still, they are discrete. Figure it out. Start with the tribe.

She closed her eyes and thought of her family. There were so many of them, wild and unpredictable and always getting married and having babies. Four brothers, six nephews, twelve nieces, a hundred cousins. Only Anna was childless.

The day before she had stood in her brother's living room watching her beautiful fourteen-year-old niece practicing a dance for her school variety show. "LIVING IN THE MATERIAL WORLD," Madonna was coming out of four speakers. "I'M LIVING IN THE MATERIAL WORLD AND I AM A MATERIAL GIRL." The beautiful niece stopped after the chorus and held out her hands toward her aunt. She was a shimmering hopeful girl, smiling a wonderful fourteen-year-old smile. She spread wide her long white fingers. "I'm going to be throwing dollars all over the place while I do it," she said. "I might get some printed up."

Anna smiled back. She was not offended. Poor nieces and nephews. They were living in the material world, surrounded by cars and sweaters and swimming pools and shoes and jackets and coats and shirts and toys and equipment.

This particular dancing niece, however, looked as if she

might survive. "I love you," Anna said. "I think you're great."

Now she was in her kitchen making coffee and looking out the window. Her old corduroy robe was belted around her waist, her feet were in ski socks, her hips were thin and hollow from living in the city. She giggled, did a little dance of home. I'm back, she decided. I'm going to work and I'm not giving another interview of any kind or letting anybody take another picture of me. Fuck it. I'm taking that goddamn phone and putting it in the shed. I'm never answering that goddamn phone again as long as I live. She turned around and read the notes pinned to her refrigerator.

Fuck doubt, press on.

The dishes can wait.

Serve the whole.

She poured a cup of coffee, added sugar and cream, stuck some chocolate mint candies in the pocket of her robe, and went into her office. It would be many hours later before she remembered it was her birthday.

The married man, she decided, unwrapping one of the mints. I will tell the story of the married man. But how to plot it? How to make it happen? How to make it live? How to move the characters around so they bruise against each other and ring true? How to ring the truth out of the story, absolve the sadness, transmute it, turn it into art?

How to do it from the start, as the poet said. Notice everything. The stain on the ceiling. The way the candle burned all night that last night he slept with me. Scott

Joplin on the stereo. "Solace" and "Red Flower Rag" and "Jasmine Blues."

The married man had made love to Anna as if there were no tomorrow. "It's like cancer," she said to him, rolling over to feel his chest against her breasts, then back again to feel his chest against her back, keeping an eye on the clock. Romeo and Juliet, star-crossed lovers, he had actually said that to her one night. She had written it on the mirror, thinking it would make her stop loving him.

Great swamps of sentimentality stretching out in three directions behind her. In front the sea of cliché, above, the maudlin skies, nothing to breathe, not a molecule of air that hasn't carried a million love songs from one radio station to another. Dance with Me, I Just Called to Say I Love You, Sail Away to Key Largo, Yes, It's Me and I'm in Love Again. Love Letters Straight from My Heart. We need Madonna, Anna thought. We need anything we can get. Anything anyone can teach us.

II

The married man had entered Anna's life at a party given by her editor in Brooklyn. A dinner party with rare roast beef and triple chocolate cake and cold spinach soup. Anna had arrived late. Her plane had fallen from the sky over Washington and made an emergency landing in New Jersey. For seven minutes the DC-9 had fallen from the sky at a severe angle of descent. Anna had breathed through an oxygen mask and wondered if she would die on impact or live to feel the skin burn from her body. *The Assumption,* she had been thinking. *Little Easters, Coming Over Jordan, Calvin Street, Psalm and Dream, Mariana.* She chanted the names of her books. She saw her unfinished manuscripts lying on her table and the new one that was put to bed in Boston waiting for the fall. Then the plane leveled off and made its bumpy landing.

"You never thought of God?" The man beside her at the dinner table unfolded his napkin and placed it on his lap. It was five hours later. Anna was sitting at her editor's dinner table. Her editor's gorgeous actress wife beamed at her. Her editor's good-looking blond son poured the wine. They were so glad she was here. So glad she was safe. The tall redheaded baby doctor was unfolding his napkin across his knee and asking if she had thought of God. His hands were beautiful and clean and freckled, like her own. Anna stared at his freckles. Ever since she had gotten off the plane her vision had been very intense, everything standing out in brilliant demarcations and colors. The tablecloth, the wineglass half full of red wine, the baby doctor's freckled hands, his immaculate fingernails, his freckled nose. His hair, the exact color of her own. She smiled at him. She believed she had known him forever.

"No," she said. "I don't believe in God. I believe in man."

"Hmmmm," he said. He smiled deeper into her face, completely caught up in her. It occurred to Anna that the whole table must be watching them. It was too thick. She shook it off.

"I've never entertained the idea of God in my life. When I was a very small child the idea seemed ludicrous and stupid and I never believed it no matter how many hours I spent on my knees at the Episcopal church. I didn't trust the ministers. And I didn't like the idea of hell and I never put my money in the collection plate. The only thing I hated worse than ministers were the men passing the collection plate." She paused, then went on. "I did find out one very interesting thing on that plane ride. I discovered

it's all right to die if you've done your work. I was saying
the titles of my books over and over to myself." She looked
at her editor. He smiled back. "Anyway, I said the titles of
the books over to myself like a mantra, then I regretted not
having children, then I was ready to die. It was all right. It
really was. It seemed all right." She sat back. The baby
doctor was still entranced. Well, he could take it or leave it.
The whole thing. The wide brow, the scary, flaky intelli-
gence.

"We never had children either," the baby doctor said.
"My wife always wanted to adopt a child but I wouldn't let
her."

"Oh, you're married," Anna said. They all laughed. Her
editor's son caught her eye. They began to talk of other
things. The party wore on to its conclusion. The baby doctor asked if she would share a cab and she said yes. She was
full of wine and at four o'clock that afternoon she had seen
her death so she took the baby doctor off to hear jazz in the
Village and later she took off her raincoat and then her
dress and took him to bed. So it began. It was everybody's
luck that his wife was out of town.

"It's a good thing I learned my lesson about married men
years ago," she said, sitting up in bed, watching him dress.
The light was coming in around the edges of the drapes. It
was a tall, old-fashioned hotel room. She had stayed there
with both her husbands. Now she was here with this married man. This freckled, redheaded baby doctor, with his
lanky bones and long, clean, immaculate freckled hands
and his surprising libido and his gentleness. "I can tell
you're a married man," she said. "Because you know how
to make love. I have a theory that the only way to learn to
make love is to be married a long time to one person. I've

been meaning to do a piece about it if I ever get time." She pulled the bedspread up around her legs, settled her elbows on her knees, looked nice and normal and balanced and uninvolved. He buttoned his pants and zipped them up. He put on his tie without looking in the mirror. He was looking at her.

"I'll call you later," he said. "Where will you be?"

"God knows. I could be anywhere. I'll probably go by my agent's or the Metropolitan Museum of Art. It's my favorite place in New York City."

"I want to see you tonight." He sat down on the bed. He put his hands on her feet. His face was as clear and unmasked as one of the two-year-olds he treated. "I'm going to fall in love with you," he said. "It's already happened. It's already too late. Don't look away. You feel it too. I know you do."

"How old are you?"

"I'm forty-five years old. I don't do this, Anna. I don't cheat on my wife. This is brand-new."

"Well, I cheat on everyone," she said. She rolled off the side of the bed. She picked up the red silk shirt she had been wearing the night before and put it on. She stood before him with her gorgeous legs, playing it for all it was worth and denying it at the same time. "And I'm not having an affair with a married man. That is that." She moved into the bathroom and began to brush her teeth, talking around the toothpaste. "If you want to take me out to dinner, get a divorce and call me up. I've done that already." She spit out the toothpaste and wiped her mouth off with a towel. He had followed her. He was watching her. "I love myself too much to have an affair with a married man." She began to floss her teeth. "Stop liking me. I don't want you to like me."

"I can't get a divorce. She's mine. I love her. I take care of her."

"Well, that's your life then, isn't it?" She pulled the dental floss out of her teeth and threw it into the sink and went back into the room and opened the drapes and looked out on Fifth Avenue. "What a city. I tried to live here once but it didn't work. I might try again. A friend offered me an apartment for next winter. Where do you live? In what part of all this."

"Near the park. You could come see me if you go to the museum. You could come by my office and see where I work." He was offering her everything he could think of. He had never in his life wanted anything as much as he wanted this woman to see him again. It made no sense and he didn't try to make sense out of it. He wanted to know everything she had ever done and was going to do. He wanted to talk to her for hours, ask her a million questions. He had read the books before he met her and seen the photographs. She was more than the sum of the parts. She was so soft, so easy to reach. He stood away from the bed with his hands at his sides waiting for her to dismiss him.

"It wasn't even all that good," she said. "I'm not very good at making love anymore. I don't get excited like I used to. I think I'm bored with the whole thing."

"It was good." He put his hands in his pockets.

"Yes," she said. "It was good." He sat down on the bed and took her back into his arms. He held her there. "Anna, please see me tonight."

"All right. If you put it that way I will. I shouldn't, but I will." Then he took off his clothes and made love to her some more and then they were really in for it.

*   *   *

They went to dinner in a small restaurant on Madison Avenue. Afterwards they walked around the city talking of their pasts. Nothing they said now made any difference. Now it was too late for words. Now they were caught up, trapped, held. She took him to a bookstore on Madison Avenue where people knew her and kept her books in the window. She wanted it seen. She wanted it validated in the world.

He took her to his apartment and showed her where he slept with his wife. The apartment was white and green, like a greenhouse, the apartment was desperately cheerful.

"Where is she?"

"She's visiting her mother."

"When will she be back?"

"This weekend."

"Good. I'm leaving Saturday."

"When will you be back?"

"This winter, but not to see you. This is only for this week."

"You can't mean that."

"Of course I mean it. You're married. You couldn't even spend the night. To hell with it. It makes me mad to even think of it. It's terrible. It's the worst thing anyone can do. The worst and stupidest and most tragic fucking thing a woman can do. I am not going to do it."

"You are doing it."

"I'm going to stop." Then she took off her coat and made love to him in his wife's bed.

"Why did we do this?" she said later.

"Because the unconscious calls the shots."

"Not in my life it doesn't." She got out of bed and began to put on her clothes. "It's two days old and already we're crazy. Well, it isn't going to happen to me. I spent five years of my life on a married man and I'm never doing it again. The last time I married a perfectly nice human being on the rebound and ruined his life. I don't want this. I'm bailing out before it's too late."

"It's too late now. It's happened."

"No, it's not. When I'm gone it will go away. I'm going to get a plane reservation and leave tomorrow. I'm getting out of here."

So Anna flew back to the mountains and it was nine months before she came back to New York City and it had done no good. The minute she saw the redhaired baby doctor it was exactly the same. Nothing had changed, not a freckle on his hand.

"It's life," he said. "Abundance, largess. You can't turn this down."

"It's a lot of bullshit," she answered. "If you like me so much, get a divorce."

"I love her."

"I don't believe you."

"Believe me. I want you to believe that so you won't get hurt."

"I'm already hurt. You're going to ruin my life for five years. It's the worst thing that ever happened to me. It's worse than the last time. It's like a groove I've worn in my brain."

"Come go to the park with me. Come see the castle they're redoing."

"It's not your fault. I'm not blaming you. I'm not blaming it on anyone. And I don't want to see the castle. Then I'd never be able to see a goddamn castle without thinking of you."

"It's my fault."

"Maybe it is. Goddammit, I was married and I got a divorce so that the next time I fell in love I'd be free to live with whomever I fell in love with. I'm not married. I'm free. Or whatever wiggle on space our small amount of freedom in the world consists of. Randolph says it's a wiggle in the petri dish. Maybe he's right. I was free until I fell in love with you. Until that plane fell from the sky and reminded me I was mortal."

"I'm sorry."

"No, you aren't. You love it."

"Go to the park and see the castle."

"Okay. I will."

That is how it went between them in the fall and winter when Anna was in New York City to have a reward and a change of scenery to liven up her work. The worst part was making sure the redhaired doctor was suffering as much as she was. She wanted him miserable. She thought she had every right to lie in bed and send him terrible messages across the city and hope they kept him up all night and made him drink.

III

Where was will in all of this? the married man wondered. He was waiting for a traffic light. It was raining. A dark evening in the rain. He was driving along Fifth Avenue. He turned on 65th into the hospital parking lot and gave the car to an attendant. He went into an office and called her apartment but the line was busy. Who was she, after all? he wondered. This woman who was doing this to him. With her short red hair as thin as a child's and her four pairs of glasses and her legs that fell apart beneath him as if there were no bones in them. "Don't read the books," she had told him. "Promise not to read my books."

It was a quirk that he never admitted he had read them. He had read them all before he knew her and one weekend he read them all again. Not that he learned anything from them. Not that they had anything to do, really, with the hand that lay across his leg or face or hand. He was not sleeping well.

Anna walked through the Metropolitan Museum of Art and stood for a long time before the half-built replica of the Parthenon trying to find some solace in the cold wisdom of the Greeks. She had been crying and it was certain that before the day was over she would cry again. She examined the gods on the frieze, in their passions and their furies. The Furies, she decided, I am being pursued by the Furies for wishing his goddamn wife was dead. To hell with it. I'm going out and buy some clothes or read a book or get drunk. That's it. I'll get drunk and get thrown in jail and he'll have to come and bail me out.

She left the museum and walked down to her favorite bookstore, a place on Madison between 81st and 82nd. Her friends were behind the counter. "How's it going?" they said. "How's life treating you?"

"Get me some books," she answered. "I need all the books I can carry. I need some books like a victim of the plague." They loaded her up with books to read, thinking she was suffering from fame.

IV

Thirteen blocks away from where Anna was trudging home through the city carrying her books the married man removed the needle from the baby's aorta and closed the incision. He wiped the blood from the arm. He handed the sponge to his assistant. He took off the great microscopic glasses and laid them on a table and looked down at the small thing that had been an eight-month-old baby boy until a moment ago. He gave an order to the nurse and walked out to the sink and pulled the gown off and washed his arms and got into his shirt and tie and suit and changed shoes and went out into the waiting room to tell the family. He waited with his hands folded while the mother consoled the father and the grandmothers held each other and the brother pulled the magazines down off a table. It was seven-fifteen in the evening of a cold wet December day. She would be gone by the time he got there and besides, she had told him not to come to her apartment or call her on the phone.

"You did what you could," the father said. The father patted his arm. The father looked into his eyes. "I thank you for trying."

"We don't get to keep them all," he told the father. "No matter what we do. I wish it wasn't so." What difference does it make? he told himself. What the fuck difference does any of it make? They ought to let the sick ones die at birth. Like the Swedes. Dip them in a bucket of cold water and the ones that lived got to live. To hell with it. He took the man's hand and removed it from his sleeve. "I have to be somewhere where someone needs me. I'm sorry I can't stay."

"It's all right," the mother said. "It's not your fault. There was nothing you could do." He made his escape before she began crying again. Walked out the side door and across the street and the parking attendant got out his car and he slid into the driver's seat and began driving aimlessly down Fifth Avenue, then around the park, then down Lexington, then up Madison to 72nd. He parked the car illegally before a brownstone and got out and walked to her building and went in and rang the bell. "Please see me."

"Come on up. I look like hell." She was right. She did look like hell. She had on a white sweatshirt and some warm-up pants and a pair of white socks and her hair was flying all over her head. "What are you doing?" he said.

"I'm writing. What's wrong with you?"

"Nothing."

"Yes there is. Tell me."

"It's nothing. Nothing anyone can do. I miss you. That's the main thing." She went over to the fireplace and began to wad up pages of newsprint and throw them into the catch. She threw in four or five wadded-up pages, then added a whole section, then put two logs on top of that. She struck a match and the mess miraculously caught and began to flame. "This wood's incredible," she said. "I think they pump lighter fluid into it. So," she turned back to where he was watching her. "Sit down. Why did you have to see me if nothing's wrong?"

"I lost a baby."

"That's nice."

"Have you had dinner?"

"No."

"Go out with me." She poked at the fire some more. It blazed higher. She left the room. In a minute music came on. "I'll order something from the deli," she said. "I don't want to get dressed. Fix a drink. I'll set the table. Go on, let's play house. We'll be married people. You'll come home from a hard day where the babies die and I'll be groping around in an old sweatshirt and what the hell, we'll make a fire and eat and make love and go to bed and sleep and get up ready to face the world again. What do you want? They have some pretty good lobster salad if you like it."

"Anything will do. That's fine." He went into the dining room and poured a glass of scotch and carried it back to the sofa. He sank back against her embroidered pillows. She went to him and sat on her knees on the floor. She ran her hands up his legs and lay her head on his lap. "I love you," she said. "If that matters."

"It matters."

"We'll eat," she said. "Then we can cry."

He spent the night. The next day was Sunday. They lay in bed all morning. They listened to the radio and made love and only cried once. They looked at each other and they were crying and they didn't talk about it. What good does it do to talk about crying?

"We could go for a walk," he said. "We could see if my car's been towed away."

"You've got a car?"

"I had one last night."

"Would you let me drive it? I haven't driven a car since I got to New York City. I need to drive a car." She was laughing now. "You don't have a tape deck, do you?"

"I think there's one. I've never used it."

"Oh, God, that would make my day. If I could drive around New York listening to music I'd get well. I keep thinking this goddamn depression isn't about you at all, it's about missing my car." She was making up the bed and talking. When she was happy she looked sixteen. Then, suddenly, she would look her age. This year, for the first time in her life she sometimes looked old. She would pass a mirror and see it and it made her curious, as if it were some stranger she was observing, something far away and foreign to herself. Now, chattering and pulling on a pale blue sweater, she seemed sixteen and not a day older. She tucked the bedspread in around the pillows. He went into the next room and called his wife.

Anna listened. She had forgotten he was married. She had broken the first and most important rule she lived by, to always know exactly where she was and what she was doing. It was the ground of her existence, the stand she made. As long as I know exactly what is going on and who I am, she told herself. As long as I don't lie to myself or to them. As long as I know. As long as the cards are on the table. As long as I call it by its name. Now, here, in this old apartment in this cold city on this dark cold December weekend, she had forgotten.

Adultery. Pandora's box. You open it and all the Furies come flying out, jealousy, rage, pain and sorrow, all the shades and Furies of the world. They flew out now, lit upon the dresser, laughed down at her from the sconces and the chandelier.

He came back into the room. "Let's walk in the park," he said. "I'd like so much to walk with you."

The car was there but she didn't want to drive it now. They went into the park which was filled with people in bright scarves and gloves. They walked for a while, then came to rest on a bench beside a statue of a Polish general on horseback.

"Will you leave her?" Anna said.

"I can't. What would she do?"

"Well, that's that then. Let's get some breakfast. I'm starving."

"I can't leave her."

"Don't talk about it anymore. I don't want to hear it. Shut up."

*   *   *

That was the absolutely last time. When she said good-bye that afternoon she meant it. Still, there were obligations to be met. It would be three more weeks before she could leave the city. She began to dream of home. She dreamed of her grandmother's farm, the long fields of milo and wheat. She dreamed his wife was in the middle of a field of wheat. Crows were all around her on the ground. She was feeding the crows from her hand. She was so gentle, so real. At least I never saw her, Anna thought. At least I was spared that.

That afternoon she ran into them at the Metropolitan beside the Greek and Roman statues. They stopped beside a huge black marble statue of a hero. The woman was very thin, very pretty, with alabaster skin. A cashmere shawl around her shoulders. There were introductions. The Greek hero looked down at them, holding his arrows and his bow.

"Have lunch with us," the woman said. "Phil has told me so much about you. We've loved your books. Do have lunch."

"I can't today," she said. "I'm researching something. For an article."

"In antiquities? I used to know a bit about them. What are you writing?"

"Oh, nothing very interesting. Just research. I'm sorry I can't stay. It's good to meet you. I have to go now. Good-bye, Philip. It's nice to see you. I mean, thank you. I'm sorry I can't stay." She escaped and went out into the sunshine and began to walk as fast as she could with her hands stuffed down into the pockets of her coat. Fists of hands, she was thinking. A fist of a heart. Yes, they were right to think it is the heart. It knots up and beats against itself and takes your breath away. Breathe, walk, run, as fast as you can down this cobbled street.

Museums went by, people in thick coats and bright Yankee hats. Anna walked all the way to 120th Street. The knot began to slacken in her breast. She stopped on a corner where a man was roasting chestnuts. His blackened jacket and his blackened face belonged to another century. A crow lit upon a bench. The sun fell between the buildings. Fuck love, she said to herself. How dare he do this to me? How did I get into this? Where am I? What on earth am I doing? It's too goddman much. I won't stay in this town another day. I'm going home. This time for good.

V

There is a way to organize this knowledge, Anna decided. To understand what happened. This love affair, this very last love affair. In a minute I will get out of this bed and begin to understand what happened. I will pick up the telephone and call Arthur and then I will begin to write the stories and they will tell me what is going on.

I will create characters and they will tell me my secrets. They will stand across the room from me with their own voices and dreams and disappointments. I will set them going like a fat gold watch, as Sylvia said. I am in my house on the mountain and I will call Daniel and Judith and Matthew and Will and Ginny and Jim. I will gather my tribe around me and celebrate my birthday. There will be champagne and a doberge cake from the bakery that Cajun runs on the highway. Yes, all that for later. For now, the work before me, waiting to be served and believed in and done. My work. How I define myself in the madness of the world.

Anna rose from the bed and turned off the electric blanket and picked up all her clothes and threw them on the closet floor and went upstairs and opened a brand-new box of 25-percent cotton bond and set it on a table by her type-writer. She pushed her hair out of her face and began to write.